Some universities have also set up entrepreneurship courses for special groups, such as women and minorities. At Imperial University of Technology, there is an entrepreneurship education and competition program for female students—We Innovate. This program was launched in 2014 with the support of The Althea Foundation and Alexsis de Raadt St. James. The Althea Foundation is a social charity investment organization. Students participating in the program will propose and improve business plans through a series of workshops, with expert lectures and one-on-one tutoring. After the program, all students can compete in WE Innovate, held every year, with the maximum prize of 10,000 pounds. As an example, a few years ago, a female Ph.D. in Environmental Engineering won the championship and her idea was to reuse waste materials to make waterproof concrete additives.

In addition, the British government has already started training programs for micro, small, and medium-sized businesses, and entrepreneurship services and support programs for specific groups. For example, the British government launched the World-First Growth Vouchers (GVP) program in early 2014 to provide professional business advice and guidance for micro, small, and medium-sized businesses. As of the end of the program, more than 28,000 micro, small, and medium-sized businesses have participated in the program. X-Forces, a cooperative organization of Start Up Loan, began to pay special attention to veterans' venture loans as early as 2013. The UK Department for Business, Innovation and Skill, National Offender Management Service, and Start Up Loans Company started their cooperation from 2014 to provide former prisoners with trainings on entrepreneurship and business plan. At present, these projects are in regular operation.

FAIR COMPETITION FOR SMEs

The regulation on the protection of SMEs in the UK competition law is indirectly or directly reflected in two aspects: "regulation on monopoly agreements" and "regulation on abuse of market dominance".

In the UK, fixed price agreements are considered to be the most harmful of all restrictive competition agreements, and the principle of illegality per se is applied, while most vertical agreements are loosely regulated.

The UK usually divides the abuse of market dominance into over-pricing, price discrimination, predatory pricing, refusal to deal, tied sale, and so on. The most obvious abusive behavior is considered to be "the pricing of enterprises with a dominant position in the market, beyond the normal price under competitive conditions, and demand high prices from the industry downstream subjects"; for the same transaction using different trading conditions, thereby putting some counterparties in a disadvantageous competitive position is discriminatory behavior. Predatory pricing refers to the sale of goods or services below cost by a dominant market player with the purpose of crowding out competitors. Tied sale is when a seller, through contractual provisions or other means, requires a buyer to purchase one or more goods or services at the same time when offering a good or service to a buyer. Refusal to deal is seller's refusal to sell goods or provide services to a specific buyer (including a retailer or wholesaler).[5]

---

[5] Price Supervision Bureau of National Development and Reform Commission. Report on Competition Policy Training in the UK. Price Supervision and Anti-monopoly in China: No. 11, 2016.

United States

The US government emphasizes the efficiency and flexibility of service to reduce the administrative burdens on SMEs. Following the Regulation Flexibility Act of 1980 and the Paper Work Reduction Act, the US government passed the Regulatory Accountability Act (2017) in early 2017, aimed at reducing red tape in government departments and promoting employment, innovation, and economic growth. As part of the Office of Commercial and Business Affairs (CBA) of the Department of State, the Global Entrepreneurship Program (GEP) seeks to promote entrepreneurship and stimulate innovation by coordinating government programs for the private sector and supporting entrepreneurs around the world. The 8th Global Entrepreneurship Summit (GES 2017) was held in India in November 2017. In March 2017, the White House Office of American Innovation (OAI) was set up and reports directly to the US President on improving government services, efficiency, and innovation, and promoting employment.

The Tax Cuts and Jobs Act effective in January 2018 reduced the maximum corporate income tax rate from 35 to 21%, which is another incentive after the Small Business Jobs Act of 2010 reduced the tax of 14 billion US dollars for small businesses. The US government coordinates the commercial loan department to provide financing support for entrepreneurs and SMEs. In addition, a specialized commercial banking system and venture capital firms are important financing sources. In view

© The Author(s), under exclusive license to Springer Nature Singapore Pte Ltd. 2022
J. Gao et al., *G20 Entrepreneurship Services Report*,
https://doi.org/10.1007/978-981-16-6787-9_21

of the contradiction between the high financing cost of start-ups and the low financing scale of the capital market, the US government widened the channel for small businesses to connect with the capital market to make it easier for small businesses to obtain the capital they need to grow. On the basis of the Jumpstart Our Business Startups (JOBS) Act in 2012, the US government passed Chapter 3 of the JOBS Act in October 2015.

The US government promotes innovation and R&D through the Small Business Innovation Research (SBIR) and Small Business Technology Transfer (STTR) that support technology transfer innovation in universities and giving high priority to small manufacturing enterprises engaged in network security research. The Small Business Administration (SBA), the US Patent and Trademark Office (USPTO), and other government agencies, as well as many other small business service agencies provide information services for small businesses.

The US government supports the market expansion of SMEs through government procurement and export promotion. The Clarity for America's Small Contractors Act of 2017, passed in July 2017 emphasizes the openness and transparency of government procurement to ensure that small businesses are fairly treated. The main purpose of the Small Business Payment for Performance Act of 2017 (HR 2594) submitted to the House of Representatives by the Small Business Committee in the same year is to ensure the timely payment to small businesses in government procurement. The Small Business Act stipulates that federal agencies should give special consideration to small businesses in government procurement. In addition, the Federal Procurement Regulations specify the reservation system for small businesses. Moreover, the Veterans Entrepreneurship and Small Business Development Act of 1999 provides the percentage of government procurement that should be contracted with service-disabled veteran-owned SMEs. According to the Small Business Export Enhancement Act, the US government has formulated a small business export promotion plan, which is specifically implemented by the SBA. In terms of business incubation services, the United States provides favorable conditions for entrepreneurship by creating science and technology parks and providing innovation and entrepreneurship spaces.

At present, some US higher education institutions have incorporated compulsory entrepreneurship education into the curriculum system. Increasing US universities are offering entrepreneurship education to students in all departments. The United States has also incorporated entrepreneurship education into the basic education, and most states have drawn up a syllabus in the K12 education system. The US women's entrepreneurship education and training are also making progress. The US entrepreneurial culture is typical, in which the role model encourages entrepreneurs to innovate or start their own businesses.

The American anti-trust law has provisions for the protection of SMEs in regulating enterprise merger (including horizontal and vertical merger). In the market with low concentration, the strength gap between large enterprises and SMEs is not very big. At this time, SMEs have the ability to compete freely, and the merger behavior in this market is rarely controlled. On the issue of exemption from monopoly agreements of SMEs, the U.S. Antitrust Guidelines for Collaborations among Competitors has made provisions on collaborations among competitors.

GOVERNMENT SERVICES

At the end of 2016, the United States passed the American Innovation and Competitiveness Act. The Act covers topics such as expansion of basic research, reduction of the administrative burdens on projects funded by the federal government, enhancement of science, technology, engineering, mathematics (STEM) education, innovation of private sectors and manufacturing sector, acceleration of technology transfer, and commercialization.

For expanding basic research, the Act reiterates the performance-based review requirements of the National Science Foundation (NSF), emphasizing that sustained and predictable federal funding for basic research is essential to maintaining the US' leading position in science and technology. In addition, it increased transparency and accountability of the NSF. Research projects financed by the federal funds shall indicate their objectives in the public notice in the manner that is easy for technical or non-technical audiences to understand, in order to promote the public understanding and confidence in financing the basic research. Moreover, the Act reiterates the US government's support for the "Established Program to Stimulate Competitive Research" (EPSCoR).

In terms of encouraging innovation in the private sector, the Science Price Competition Act updated the authorization of innovation awards, amended relevant contents of the Stevenson-Wydler Technology Innovation Act of 1980, and gave the federal government more flexibility in setting up science competition awards, including bonus sources. This part of content also stipulates that federal scientific institutions can advance their tasks through crowdsourcing or cooperation with the US citizens who are willing to engage in that. It authorizes the National Institute of Standards and Technology (NIST) to be the "chief adviser to the US president on the national standard policy related to scientific and technological competitiveness and innovation capability".

In terms of commercialization and technology transfer, the Act allows researchers, students, and other institutions funded by other federal agencies than the NSF to participate in the Innovation Corps Program (I-Corps) of the NSF. Women entrepreneurs should be supported through guidance, education, training, and investment to build a strong innovation system. The NSF is required to provide funding for I-Crops program participants. In addition, the Act requires the NFS to continue to provide funding for other eligible entities in order to promote the commercialization of results of researches funded by the federal government. The American Innovation and Competitiveness Act aims to: (1) improve the US competitiveness, (2) create jobs, (3) stimulate the development of new business and industrial opportunities, and (4) provide a policy basis for the US government to invest in basic research.

In serving SMEs, the US government has been placing a priority on the efficiency and flexibility of service to reduce the administrative burdens on SMEs. The US government passed the Regulatory Accountability Act (2017) in early 2017, aimed at reducing red tape in government departments, cutting unnecessary and tedious regulations, and promoting employment, innovation, and economic growth. In fact, the US government promulgated the Regulatory Flexibility Act of 1980 and the Paper Work Reduction Act in 1980. Under the Regulatory Flexibility Act of 1980 (RFA or Reg Flex Act), government departments are required to review alternatives that can reduce burdens. If federal regulations and rules have a significant impact on most small businesses, the creativity, productivity, and competitiveness of small businesses will not be affected while realizing the management objectives.

The Regulatory Accountability Act of 2017 contains six independent reform acts, one of which is the Small Business Regulatory Flexibility Improvements Act that specifically targets small businesses. It amended the RFA and the Small Business Regulatory Enforcement Act of 1996 (SBREFA). It also amended and expanded provisions and procedures of federal agencies to amend laws and regulations relating to small businesses. Government agencies are required to seek flexible solutions and improve service efficiency and flexibility by fully considering the direct,

UNITED STATES 279

indirect, and long-term impact of the formulation and release of laws and regulations. For example, the Act requires federal agencies to submit detailed analysis reports on the purpose, legal basis, type, quantity, and scope of small businesses that may be affected, and on any laws and regulations that have an unreasonable impact, especially economic impact, on small businesses. Plans should be devised to regularly review existing and new rules.

The Paper Work Reduction Act (PRA) requires the federal government to submit the request for collecting all information to the Office of Information and Regulatory Affairs (OIRA) before collecting information from the public. The PRA requires the OIRA to approve the reporting and recording requirements only if necessary or required by law so as to minimize the paperwork burdens on individuals and small businesses.

The partial function of the Office of Commercial and Business Affairs (CBA) of the US Department of State is to promote entrepreneurship. As part of the CBA of the US Department of State, the Global Entrepreneurship Program (GEP) seeks to promote entrepreneurship and stimulate innovation by coordinating government programs for the private sector and supporting entrepreneurs around the world. In the spirit of spreading the American entrepreneurial culture, the GEP was launched in April 2010 at the Presidential Summit on Entrepreneurship.

The GEP supports the establishment of an integrated entrepreneurial ecosystem and highlights seven key areas of entrepreneurial development: identification, training, connection and maintenance, directing financing, facilitating market access, supportive policies, and motivating entrepreneurs. GEP partners include domestic and global NGOs, companies, foundations, educational institutions, and investors. Partner organizations are required to extend the current entrepreneurship program to a new country or deepen their existing entrepreneurship programs.

The specific activities of the GEP include:

Global Entrepreneurship Summits (GES). It connects US entrepreneurs and investors with their international peers, creates new opportunities for cooperation and forms lasting relationships, and emphasizes entrepreneurship as a means to address some of the most difficult global challenges. The GES usually includes a series of extensive seminars, group discussions, lectures, competitions, tutoring and networking meetings to provide participants with targeted opportunities to acquire skills and social relationships to help their businesses develop.

The GES 2017 was held in Hyderabad, India, in November 2017 with the theme of "Women First, Prosperity for All".

Global Entrepreneurship Week (GEW). November is the National Entrepreneurship Month in the US. It is a festival to celebrate entrepreneurs who serve the community and support the US economy. During a week of every November, US embassies and consulates organize events to promote and inspire the US overseas entrepreneurship.

Mexico-US Entrepreneurship and Innovation Council (MUSEIC). The Council's mission is to promote and strengthen cross-border design and innovation systems so as to improve cross-border production systems. MUSEIC has seven subcommittees to advance the pillars that make up the Council's Mission: (1) providing a legal framework that encourages innovative entrepreneurship; (2) promoting women entrepreneurship; (3) engaging entrepreneurs among the Latin American diaspora residing in the US; (4) promoting and integrating the infrastructure supporting entrepreneurs and Small and Medium Enterprises; (5) sharing expertise and best practices to develop regional innovation clusters and marketing chains; (6) exchanging best practices on technology commercialization; and (7) sharing tools and best practices on financing and promoting innovative and high-impact entrepreneurship. The Council is comprised of 24 leaders in the high-impact entrepreneurship field, 12 from either country, for example representatives from government, academia, NGOs, the private sector, business accelerators, and angel/venture capital funds, including the US Department of State and the National Entrepreneurship Institute (INADEM).

In March 2017, the United States set up the White House Office of American Innovation (OAI). The OAI reports directly to President Trump and submits policy and plan recommendations to the president on improving government services and efficiency, innovation, and employment promotion.

Fiscal and Financial Support

The US government introduced the Tax Cuts and Jobs Act at the end of 2017 and officially implemented it in January 2018, aiming to expand employment, stimulate investment, and promote economic development through tax reform measures such as simplifying the tax system and reducing tax rates. The Act changed the eight-tier progressive tax rate of federal corporate income tax (the average tax rate of large companies is about 35%) to a single tax rate of 21%, and imposes no corporate income tax on SMEs within the prescribed scope, but individual income tax. After the US government introduced the tax reform plan, some G20 member states also started to introduce their own tax cut plans. For example, the British government announced to cut the corporate tax rate to 17% by 2020, while the Indian government has introduced tax cut plans for individuals and SMEs, as well as tax reduction and reform. The US government's Tax Cuts and Jobs Act of 2017 is an important measure after the Small Business Jobs Act of 2010 that introduced up to 14 billion US dollars in tax cuts, credits and other incentives for small businesses to promote economic growth and create jobs.

The US government coordinates the US commercial loan department to provide financing support for entrepreneurs and SMEs by authorizing the SBA. In addition, there is a commercial banking system specialized in serving SMEs.

The SBA helps small businesses to obtain funds in the following forms:

1. 7(a) Loan Program. About 6000 commercial banks in the United States can provide loans guaranteed by the SBA, with a single limit of 5 million US dollars, and SBA can guarantee up to 90% of loans.
2. CDC/504 Loan Program. The SBA provides long-term loans for growing small businesses for major fixed assets such as land and buildings through a registered development company (CDC), with a single limit of 5 million US dollars. 504 Loans are in cooperation with private lending institutions, who has a priority lien of up to 50% on assets, while the CDC has a sub lien of up to 40%. The borrowing enterprises have no less than 10% of their own funds. The CDC's contribution to the 504 loan is 100% guaranteed by the SBA.
3. Microloan Program. The SBA cooperates with non-profit loan agencies to provide small businesses with small loans of no more than 50,000 US dollars.
4. Small Business Investment Company (SBIC) Program. The SBIC program provides venture capital and start-up capital for small businesses. SBIC is a private investment company approved, supervised, and partially funded by SBA.

The United States has a commercial banking system that specializes in serving SMEs. For example, Silicon Valley Bank provides basic loans and savings, as well as business services such as venture capital and investment banking. Community banks, small commercial banks serving SMEs within their jurisdictions, have the same basic business as large commercial banks, but their loans are small, mainly providing "relational loans" for SMEs in that they have closer ties with SMEs and can provide more stable financing for SMEs. Unlike the online small business lending institutions of commercial banks, these professional institutions provide unsecured loans for small businesses, usually with a small amount of funds not exceeding 50,000 US dollars.

Venture capital is an important financing source for start-up and SMEs. According to Money Tree Report released by PricewaterhouseCoopers and the NVCA, there were 5427 US venture capital transactions in 2017, with a turnover of 73.8 billion US dollars. Venture capital mainly flows to early enterprises (24.8%), expansion enterprises (19.9%), seed enterprises (29.3%), and mature enterprises (9.5%). By average transaction size, seed enterprises received 6.9 million US dollars, early enterprises 24.6 million US dollars, expansion enterprises 64 million US dollars, and mature enterprises 112 million US dollars.

The United States has a more mature NVCA as a platform for information communication and education popularization. The US Angel Capital Association (ACA) serves as a connecting platform between angel investors and start-ups, helping start-ups find angel investment teams, and providing investment guidance and education for angel investors. As members of the Association, venture capital enterprises may receive education, research, and mutual contact services. At the same time, the Association provides policy advice for the government.

In view of the contradiction between the high financing cost of start-ups and the low financing scale of the capital market, the US government released the JOBS Act in 2012 to widen channels for small businesses to connect with the capital market to make it easier for small businesses to obtain the capital they need to grow. In October 2015, it passed Chapter 3 of the JOBS Act, lifting the restriction that investors must be qualified and prescribing the ordinary investors may invest in small businesses in need of finance through crowd funding.

Chapter 3 of the JOBS Act passed in 2015 stipulates as below: if the annual income of an individual investor is less than 100,000 US dollars, the amount it may invest each year should be the greater of 2000 US dollars and 5% of their annual income; if the annual income of an individual investor is more than 100,000 US dollars, the amount it may invest each year should be 10% of its annual income or personal net assets. In addition, the maximum equity investment through crowd funding every year should be limited to 100,000 US dollars. Moreover, it is stipulated that start-ups and small businesses can raise no more than 1 million US dollars per year through private equity crowd funding.

The JOBS Act covers the identification of emerging growth companies (EGC), simplification of the IPO issuance procedures, reduction of issuance costs, and information disclosure obligations. Title IV "Regulation A" amended the provisions of Regulation A of the Securities Act of 1933 relating to exemption of microfinance from registration and increased the upper limit of amount of microfinance (which may be used for public offering) within 12 months that is exempted from registration to 50 million US dollars, which is also known as "mini IPO".

ENTREPRENEUR SERVICES

Technical Services

On the basis of laws and regulations such as the Patent and Trademark Law Amendments Act (Bayh–Dole Act), the Stevenson-Wydler Technology Innovation Act, and the Technology Transfer Commercialization Act, the US government promotes innovation and R&D through SBIR and STTR to provide technical services. In October 2017, the US government adopted the Small Business Innovation Research and Small Business Technology Transfer Improvements Act of 2017, which made necessary improvements to SBIR and STTR. For example, it requires federal agencies participating in the STTR to implement the Innovative Approaches to Technology Transfer Grant Program and supports the technology transfer and innovation of higher learning institutions. In addition, it requires to give high priority to the small manufacturers engaged in network security research, while implementing the SBIR and STTR. Moreover, it breaks down the types and amounts of technical and commercial assistance provided by the SBIR and the STTR for small business. Furthermore, it requires the SBA to submit the annual analysis reports of the SBIR and the STTR.

The SBIR is a national and permanent enterprise technology innovation campaign organized and implemented by the US government in accordance with the Small Business Innovation and Development Act passed by Congress in 1982. The SBIR is aimed at small businesses. It supports the R&D of small businesses by ensuring the federal government's investment in R&D funds and helps small businesses compete fairly with large companies. The STTR, launched in 1994, is a national program aimed at promoting joint ventures between the public and private sectors, non-profit research institutions, and small businesses to develop scientific and technological achievements. It combines the advantages of universities and research institutions with small businesses, promotes transfer of technology and products from laboratories to the market, and boosts the commercialization of scientific and technological achievements.

Information Services

In terms of information services, the SBA provides consulting services and training for SMEs from the aspects of entrepreneurship preparation, planning, company establishment, administration, and business finance. It organizes lectures and seminars, and cooperates in issuing various publications. Its online information consulting service is an important service. Information about the establishment and development of small businesses can be obtained from the SBA's website, and various problems that may be encountered in the process of establishing and operating small businesses have been compiled into standardized answers for users to inquire at any time. Many small business service organizations in the United States also provide information services for small businesses. For example, the SBDC has hired experts in law, finance, taxation, trade, management, and technology to give targeted guidance to small businesses.

Other US government departments also provide information services for entrepreneurs and SMEs. The USPTO's four regional offices in Detroit, Denver, the Silicon Valley, and Dallas began to set up special consultation hotlines for start-ups, issue detailed guidance documents, provide guidance to innovative entrepreneurs on patent and intellectual property issues, and hold a series of road shows in the United States to help entrepreneurs understand the intellectual property system. In addition, the USPTO trains young entrepreneurs on invention creation by holding summer training courses and other activities, so that junior and senior high school teachers can learn about intellectual property rights.

UNITED STATES 285

Market Support

In terms of market services, the US government supports SMEs through government procurement and export promotion.

The US House of Representatives passed the Clarity for America's Small Contractors Act of 2017 in July 2017, which emphasizes the openness and transparency of government procurement to ensure that small businesses can secure government procurement orders fairly. The main contents include requiring the SBA to list the responsibilities of procurement agencies in detail and report the value of single-source procurement contracts. The US Small Business Payment for Performance Act of 2017 (HR 2594) was submitted by the US Small Business Committee in early 2017 to partially revise the contents of the Small Business Act relating to government procurement. The draft mainly includes such contents as ensuring timely payment of government procurement to small businesses when purchase orders are changed, and payment of government procurement to secondary subcontractors and suppliers.

Under the Small Business Act, federal agencies should give special consideration to small businesses (i.e., separately listed small businesses) in terms of government procurement. The Act clearly requires that all contracts with an expected amount of 30,000–100,000 US dollars that small businesses can afford should be reserved and given to small businesses as far as possible. The portion that exceeds 100,000 US dollars should be reserved. The bidders for the federal procurement contacts of more than 500,000 US dollars should provide some subcontract opportunities to small businesses. To help small business secure more government procurement orders, the SBA set up the Office of Government Procurement, of which the main task is to maximize the opportunities for small businesses to federal procurement. The Federal Procurement Regulations also specify the small business reservation system, the small business subcontracting system and the small business offer preferential system. The Veterans Entrepreneurship and Small Business Development Act of 1999 provides that 3% of government procurement that should be contracted with service-disabled veteran-owned SMEs.

According to the Small Business Export Enhancement Act, the US government has formulated a small business export promotion plan and the SBA has set up a number of small business export assistance centers throughout the country, an export trade promotion department in the regional office of the SBA and an international trade center in the small business development center to provide legal and financial services for the export of small business products. At the same time, it also cooperates with the Department of Commerce, the Import–Export Bank, local governments, and commercial trade organizations to provide resource support for the export of small business products. For example, the SBA and banks jointly developed an online export risk analysis tool to help small businesses obtain export loans. The SBA has also signed agreements with Russia, Mexico, South Africa, and other countries on its own initiative to establish trade relations and organize small businesses to participate in product exhibitions and promotions overseas.

Enterprise Incubation

In terms of business incubation services, the United States provides favorable conditions for entrepreneurship by creating science and technology parks and providing innovation and entrepreneurship spaces, as well as special plans and funds to promote innovation and entrepreneurship.

The US government has set up high-efficiency service science parks to create favorable conditions for innovation and entrepreneurship. For example, the "Triangle Research Park" co-founded by the North Carolina government and universities, the "Austin High-tech Center" built by the Austin municipal government, and the "Silicon Slopes" in Utah have given birth to such successful cases as Domo. Domo is a smart cloud platform start-up, which is committed to providing corporate information and data services for enterprises and supports the information push and interaction across platforms and terminals. In 2015, its estimated value exceeded 2 billion US dollars.

Other states, including California's Silicon Valley, have built up space for innovation and entrepreneurship to promote entrepreneurship. For example, Utah has set up a Bio Innovation Gateway (BIG) incubator and cooperated with the University of Utah, Utah State University, and Brigham Young University to promote innovation and entrepreneurship in the life science industry. The Bio Innovation Gateway is supported by the USTAR (Utah Science Technology and Research Initiative) program jointly set up by Utah's Legislature and Governor. USTAR's main function is to support innovation and entrepreneurship, lift barriers to technology transfer, and break the market gap by connecting capital, management, and industry.

The US Department of Commerce's Clean Energy National Incubator Program has invested 3 million US dollars to support five professional incubators to help transform clean energy technologies, and has implemented a cross-national laboratory pilot program, investing 20 million US dollars to provide innovation vouchers for small businesses, which can be used by small businesses to acquire clean energy technologies.

The US government launched the "i6 Challenge" program, an innovation competition program set up by the National Institutes of Health (NIH) and the NSF with a joint investment of 12 million US dollars, aimed at promoting the entry of innovative ideas into the market by driving innovation and entrepreneurship and establishing strong public–private partnerships.

The Technology Commercialization and Innovation Program in Utah, implemented by the Utah Government Economic Development Office, provides competitive funding of up to 200,000 US dollars for innovation teams of small businesses and universities to accelerate the commercialization of innovative technologies, and aims to help businesses and teams secure funding sources at key stages of the commercialization life cycle.

South Dakota has set up a Proof of Concept Fund, which provides support of up to 25,000 US dollars for each innovative concept technology and economic feasibility study, and is applicable to entrepreneurs, universities and existing South Dakota enterprises or other entities attempting to commercialize the achievements in the state.

Digital Transformation Support

SBA was joined by a group of leading technology companies to announce the formation of the Small Business Technology Coalition, a first-of-its-kind public–private partnership that provides America's small businesses a streamlined interface to connect to innovative technology platforms as well as digital education and enterprise training. Through this coalition, the SBA collaborates with a group of the world's most iconic technology companies to educate entrepreneurs on the range of resources and technology available to help them connect to customers, scale, and do business safely anywhere. This collection of resources covers areas important to entrepreneurs including online commerce and payment platforms, efficiency of back-office operations, productivity solutions, cyber security

288   J. GAO ET AL.

protection, improved customer service and shopping experiences, which played a great role in mitigating the effect of Covid-19 in 2020 on small businesses and entrepreneurs.[1]

ENTREPRENEURSHIP EDUCATION

At present, some US higher education institutions have incorporated entrepreneurship education into the curriculum system as a compulsory course. Among the courses of entrepreneurship education in the US universities, the popular courses are Entrepreneurship, Business Planning, Entrepreneurial Finance, New Venture Creation, and Innovation. Courses such as Psychology Traits and Startup Characteristics are also valued highly among entrepreneurship courses.

Increasing US universities are offering entrepreneurship education to students in all departments. For example, the Entrepreneurship Center of the School of Engineering at Stanford University initiated the Stanford Technology Ventures Program (STVP), in cooperation with the School of Management Engineering, offers entrepreneurship courses and organizes extracurricular related activities for Stanford students. In addition, it studies influential technology start-ups and provides support for global entrepreneurship education through continuous improvement on online courses.

The University of California, Berkeley, has established the Berkeley Gateway to Innovation, which includes many processes, such as New Venture Education, Acceleration, and Funding. Institutions or programs that provide entrepreneurial education includes Berkeley–Haas Entrepreneurship Program of the School of Business, the Jacobs Institute for Design Innovation of the College of Engineering, and Intellectual Property and Industry Research Alliances (IPIRA). The university will receive government funding for entrepreneurship education, such as a grant of 2.2 million US dollars from the California government announced in December 2017, which is used for infrastructure and curriculum development.

Babson College applies the idea of entrepreneurship education to many aspects as a spirit of challenging difficulties, but not limited to starting new businesses. The college has an evaluation system for entrepreneurship

---

[1] Assessment on the progress of G20 Entrepreneurship Action Plan, Entrepreneurship Research Center on G20 Economies, Oct 22, 2019.

education, which is evaluated by teachers according to students' academic achievements.

The United States has also incorporated entrepreneurship education into the basic education. Of the 50 states in the US, 42 have already formulated syllabus in the K12 education system, and 18 have formulated the curriculum related to entrepreneurship education. The courses are largely general economics knowledge courses, and some states adopt the National Standards for Financial Literacy curriculum system developed by the Council for Economic Education. Some states (such as Arizona, California, and Arkansas) adopted their own curriculum standards, mainly focusing on the economic content of Social Studies Standards set by state education departments, including communication skills and business skills. The secondary schools (high schools) in the United States have a Career and Technical Education (CTE) which contains the entrepreneurship education.

The US women's entrepreneurship education and training are also making progress. The Secretary's Office of Global Women's Issues at the US Department of State is committed to supporting global women entrepreneurs by means of training, online education, expanding social network, and mentoring.

The Secretary's Office of Global Women's Issues at the US Department of State, the US Department of State's Office of International Information Programs, and Arizona State University's Thunderbird School of Management jointly created the DreamBuilder, a free online learning website provided for women who want to start their own businesses, which can be found at American Spaces. DreamBuilder consists of 13 courses for entrepreneurs to learn to start a business step by step. Most courses take 1–2 hours to complete. After the completion of the whole study, the students will form a complete business plan. Woman Business Centers (WBCs) is a non-profit organization with more than 100 branches throughout the country. The organization is committed to promoting women's entrepreneurship through training and technical support, and provides funding and international trading opportunities.

The US entrepreneurship culture is very typical in encouraging entrepreneurship. Among the Fortune 500 companies in 2017, there were 132 US companies, many of which are well known for their entrepreneurial stories, such as Microsoft's Bill Gates, Apple's Jobs, Google's two founders, Facebook's Zuckerberg and Amazon's Bezos. These successful entrepreneurial stories not only inspire entrepreneurs in the United States, but also entrepreneurs all over the world. There are enough role models to encourage entrepreneurs to start a business, provide experiences such as innovation and cooperation to promote entrepreneurial success, and understand the attitude of failure. Together with entrepreneurship education and training, a virtuous circle of entrepreneurship education and training, successful entrepreneurship, creation of entrepreneurial role models, acceptance of failures, and encouragement of entrepreneurship has been formed.

Fair Competition for SMEs

The American anti-trust law has provisions for the protection of SMEs in regulating enterprise merger (including horizontal and vertical merger). When the American Department of Justice's Merger Guide controls the horizontal merger behavior of enterprises, it divides the market into three categories: market with concentration trend, concentrated market, and highly concentrated market, and adopts a lenient to strict control attitude toward the merger behavior of enterprises in these three markets.

In the market with low concentration, the strength gap between large enterprises and SMEs is not very big. At this time, SMEs have the ability to compete freely, and the merger behavior in this market is rarely controlled. However, in the market with high concentration, due to the disparity in strength between SMEs and large enterprises, the merger behavior will be strictly controlled. When controlling a vertical merger, if the strength and scale of the enterprise merged by one enterprise is not as strong as the enterprise in a certain market, but the merged enterprise has a large market share in another market and occupies a dominant position in the market, the merger of the two enterprises will lead to a tilted market balance, and the merged enterprise will lose its living space because of the merger although it has good development prospects. The merged enterprise may take advantage of the opportunity to enter another market, which may cause damage to the SMEs in the other market, and such a merger is prohibited.[2]

On the issue of exemption from monopoly agreements of SMEs, the US Antitrust Guidelines for Collaborations among Competitors has made the following provisions on collaborations among competitors:

---

[2] Wang Xiaohua. Research on Competition Law [M]. China Legal Publishing House, 1999.

Except in exceptional circumstances, the competent authority will not charge a competitor with conspiracy if the combined market share of the conspiracy and its participants does not exceed twenty percent of each relevant market in which competition may be affected.

INDEX

A

Abastartup, 20, 61, 66
accredited, 175
ACSGN, 50
adjudication, 109
administrative approval, 8, 79, 84, 85
administrative burden, 2, 8, 12, 59, 62, 135, 138, 142, 153, 275, 277, 278
aerospace technology, 148
aggravated, 242
Amavulandlela, 245
AMGC, 50
angel investors, 64, 86, 90, 92, 93, 175, 256, 282
ANR, 37
anti-monopoly, 30, 108, 109, 152, 157, 203, 231
anti-trust, 5, 30, 46, 56, 112, 126, 157, 172, 179, 180, 182, 189, 190, 193, 203, 204, 220, 231, 277, 290
apprenticeship, 203
archipelagos, 165

Argentina's sectoral Argentina Fund (FONARSEC), 34, 38
Argentine Development Strategy 2017, 14, 34, 38, 39
Argentine Foreign Trade and Investment Bank (BICE), 38
Arrecado, 63
artificial intelligence, 19, 102, 129, 146, 157, 201
Askrindo, 159
ASPIR, 21
asset depreciation, 173
Association of Southeast Asian Nations (ASEAN), 120
audit control, 227
auspices, 209
authentications, 155
awareness of entrepreneurial opportunities, 76
Aziz, Abdul, 237

B

Badir Program for Technology Incubator, 234, 237
Baidu, 102

© Tsinghua University Press 2022
J. Gao et al., *G20 Entrepreneurship Services Report*,
https://doi.org/10.1007/978-981-16-6787-9

293

294 INDEX

Barclays, 269
benchmark loan interest rate, 90
beneficiaries, 255
Bengaluru, 156
Bhubaneswar, 154
bidders, 149, 285
bond market, 3, 82
Bpifance, 131
Bradesco, 63
Brandenburg, 147
Brazil, 12, 13, 22, 59–68, 120, 199
Brexit, 268
BRICS, 224
bridging loans, 245
broadband installation subsidies, 268
budgetary, 243
Buenos, 35
Buffelshoek, 250
Bulgaria, 124
bureaucratic, 114
business environment, 22, 61, 111,
   114, 121, 161, 219, 221, 264,
   271
business fair, 154

C
Capacitar, 41
capital market, 3, 13, 39, 80, 82, 87,
   90, 105, 111, 115, 117, 185,
   276, 282
cloud data, 178
Clydesdale, 269
collateral, 140, 245
commercial banking system, 205, 209,
   275, 281, 282
Confcommercio, 179
consortia, 177
conspiracy offence, 77
consulting service, 46, 48, 51, 61, 62,
   66, 72, 74, 75, 103, 121, 122,
   136, 142, 144, 146, 197, 201,
   211, 226, 255, 256, 284

corporate tax system, 11, 48
corporation tax, 263, 266
Council for Scientific and
   Technological Research
   (TUBITAK), 254, 259
counter-guarantee, 115, 117
credit guarantee system, 3, 13, 181
credit policy, 80, 91, 195
credit support, 3, 59, 62, 97
cross-border trade, 162
crowdfunding, 175, 191, 196
CSIRO Innovation Fund, 45, 47, 49
CUIT (Identification Number), 40
customization, 143

D
decentralizing, 79
decompose, 149
demographic changes, 1
Denmark, 199
Department of Innovation, Industry,
   Science and Research (DIISR),
   45
deregulation, 265
Digital Assistance Network, 41
Digital Infrastructure, 155
Digital Innovation and Scale-Up
   Initiative (DISC), 123
digitalization/digitalized, 22, 23, 46,
   53, 61, 66, 75, 99, 112, 113,
   115, 123, 140, 145, 178, 206,
   213, 262, 264, 271
digital platform, 22, 34, 41, 212,
   226, 227
digital solidarity, 172, 178
direct loan, 245
discrepancies, 30
dividend, 267
downstream, 274

E

ease of doing business (EODB), 161, 162
eBay, 197
e-commerce, 19, 20, 41, 99, 155, 163, 164, 166–168, 172, 177, 198, 212, 214, 247, 254, 258
Economic Action Plan (EAP), 73
ecosystems, 259
Ecuador/Ecuadorian, 199
e-government, 52, 59, 61, 136, 138, 142, 165
EMLYON, 25
employment assistance, 115
Empréstimo, 64
entrepreneurial community, 166
entrepreneurial ecology, 35, 43, 262
entrepreneurial environment, 2, 6, 7, 23, 31, 34, 40, 161, 206
entrepreneurial role models, 243, 251, 254, 260, 261, 290
entrepreneurial spirit, 4, 29, 67, 105, 145, 148, 169, 227, 261, 272
entrepreneurial talents, 131, 188, 189
entrepreneurial team, 96, 102, 146
entrepreneur services, 2, 3, 15, 40, 50, 64, 164, 176, 182, 211, 234, 247, 253
Entrepreneurship and Innovation Commission Mechanism, 206, 213
entrepreneurship counseling, 54, 96, 201
entrepreneurship culture, 24, 27, 61, 67, 112, 123, 147, 192, 202, 214, 243, 264, 289
entrepreneurship training program, 24, 26, 27, 34, 41, 61, 67, 68, 168, 169, 192, 201, 206, 214, 220, 229, 249, 250
enumerated, 56
e-platform, 213

Equifax, 268
equipment procurement, 60, 63
equity crowdfunding, 171, 175
equity financing, 3, 82
Escola, 69
Established Program to Stimulate Competitive Research (EPSCoR), 277
European Enterprise Promotion Awards, 254, 258
exchange platform, 3, 6, 21, 81, 98, 160, 165, 234
export assistance, 152, 285
extracurricular, 288

F

Fair competition for SMEs, 2, 5, 30, 56, 77, 108, 126, 133, 149, 157, 170, 179, 189, 203, 231, 261, 273, 290
fair trade, 108, 181, 182, 186
financing threshold, 241, 243
Fintech, 13, 60, 64, 156
fiscal support, 62, 86
FONSOFT Trust Fund, 34, 37
France, 8, 9, 16, 18, 19, 69, 127, 128, 130–133, 173, 206, 212, 215
freelance, 143

G

G20 Entrepreneurship Action Plan, 1, 2, 31, 36, 53, 123, 132, 145, 155, 167, 187, 213, 226, 271, 288
Global Entrepreneurship Program (GEP), 7, 275, 279
Go-Digital, 22, 144
government procurement, 3, 7, 17, 18, 30, 35, 45, 46, 51, 83, 137, 149, 151, 154, 181, 186, 206,

296 INDEX

211, 212, 221, 225, 264, 265, 269, 270, 276, 285
Grace Plan, 33, 36
guarantee banks, 136, 140
guarantee clauses, 140
guarantee financing, 82, 242, 246

H
Hack, 146
hatched, 212
Hatchlab, 55
HEIP, 210
Hexagon, 131
High Impact Entrepreneurship Program (HIEP), 205, 209
Hungary, 199
Hyderabad, 280
Hyundai, 198

I
iEntrepreneur, 250
IGNITE, 169
incentive, 2, 3, 11, 12, 14, 15, 35, 45, 47, 49, 60, 64, 65, 82, 84, 87, 90, 95, 105, 111, 114, 142, 151, 153, 162, 163, 173, 174, 176, 185, 191, 194, 253, 255, 261, 266–268, 275, 281
Indonesia Entrepreneur Center (IDEC), 166
industrial design, 98, 145
industrial supply chain, 1
industry-university-research cooperation, 8, 50
information asymmetry, 4
information service, 16, 51, 60, 65, 72, 74, 80, 89, 94, 118, 142, 154, 268, 276, 284
infrared, 229
infringements, 261

In-Kingdom Total Value Add (IKTVA) Program, 233, 235
innosphere, 260
Innova, 66
Innovation Act (IACT), 54
innovation and entrepreneurship education reform, 81, 100, 101
Innovation and Skills Plan, 26, 71–73, 76
Innovation Corps Program (I-Corps), 26, 207, 214, 215, 278
innovation ecosystem, 20, 25, 52, 122, 239
Innovation Law, 15, 60, 65
innovation management, 144, 145
INOVENT, 260
Intellectual Property Protection Law (1981), 35
intellectual property rights, 4, 82, 107, 120, 121, 130, 172, 176, 229, 284
interconnection, 119
inter-ministerial liaison meetings, 182, 186
International Monetary Fund (IMF), 33

J
Jamshedpur, 156
Japan External Trade Organization (JETRO), 183
Jumpstart Our Business Startups (JOBS) Act, 276
jurisprudence, 56
JUVEN, 215
Juventud, 215

K
K12 education system, 24, 277, 289
Kauffman, 148
KfW, 140

INDEX 297

King Fahd University of Petroleum
and Minerals (KFUPM), 237
KOMMIT, 143
Korea Trade Promotion Corporation
(KOTRA), 196

L
Landing Pads program, 19, 46
Lavoro, 179
learning-by-doing, 179
legal environment, 106, 130, 137,
219, 263, 265
Ley de Emprenderers, 39
low-cost, 16, 46, 51, 53, 228

M
machine learning, 157
Mafisa, 244
maker space, 96
marginalization, 215
market access, 62, 108, 113, 165, 279
market dominance, 5, 30, 46, 56, 72,
77, 112, 126, 137, 149, 157,
160, 170, 172, 179, 182, 189,
193, 203, 220, 231, 264, 273
market entry, 179
market exit mechanism, 109
Market in Financial Instruments
Regulation (MiFIR), 118
marketization, 15
market monopoly, 137
market-oriented, 15, 93, 145
market share, 30, 112, 126, 145, 150,
170, 203, 290, 291
mass entrepreneurship and innovation,
20, 21, 79–81, 83, 85, 91, 96,
100, 105
medical industry, 148
Mexico, 7, 20, 22, 26, 28, 205–212,
214–216, 286
MFI, 162

microbusiness, 184
microfinance, 111, 114–117, 164,
211, 223, 283
microloan, 281
mini IPO, 283
MIT, 260
modular, 143
mom-and-pop shops, 192, 201
momentum, 1
monopolistic behaviors, 157
monopolized, 221
Monshaat, 234, 237
Motsepe, 250
MOUs, 192
multi-certificates, 8, 79, 84
multifaceted, 99
multilateral, 50
Mumbai, 154
MYPYMES, 213

N
Nagoya, 189
NASDAQ, 196
National Development Plan (NDP),
7, 207, 241, 243
national digital ecosystem, 220, 226
National Economic Prosecutor, 205,
209
National Entrepreneurship Institute
(INADEM), 9, 26, 206–216,
280
National Innovation and Science
Agenda (NISA), 8, 47–52
National Innovation Plan 2020, 8, 33,
36
National Microenterprise Financing
Program, 206, 210
National Productivity Investment
Fund (NPIF), 16, 263, 268
National Youth Development Agency
(NYDA), 242, 244

298 INDEX

NERA, 50
nonrefundable, 37, 49
numeracy, 271
NVIDIA, 146

O
Ochanomizu, 188
OECD, 32
Open Learning Environment (OLE), 55
OTC, 91

P
Palermo, 43
parent fund, 74, 89, 136, 141, 151, 153
patenting, 144
pedagogy, 239
People's Bank of Indonesia (PBI), 160
Perdagangan, 161
Pitch@Palace, 20, 264
PlugBridge, 215
preferential income tax policy, 159
prescribed scope, 281
progressive tax rate, 280
protection on rights and interests, 10, 82, 83, 105
Public Contracts Regulations (PCRS), 269
public expenditure, 129

Q
QLD, 52

R
R&D credits, 171
R&D expenses, 86, 88
refunding, 235
regulatory burden, 114, 121, 265

reinvestment, 267
rejuvenation, 1
renovated, 94
Reuters, 56
Reverse-Direct, 19, 192, 197
revitalize, 189
revolutionizing, 155
Riyyadi, 234, 238
Russian Network Innovation and Development Fund, 220

S
Sabanci, 259
SAMADHAAN, 18
SancorSeguros, 43
SARE system, 208
Saudi Arabia, 9, 10, 234–238
Saudi Entrepreneur Program (Riyyadi), 234
SBDC, 284
Scaleup, 230
School Development Outreach (SDO), 169
Schwab, 250
Science, Technology and Innovation Framework Law (2001), 35
Scotland, 269
SEBRATE, 67
SEBTRATE, 67
Self-Employment Initiative, 27, 46, 53
SelfStart, 53
shared credit data, 17, 264
simplified business entity (SAS), 39, 40
simplified tax system, 13, 219, 222
small and medium enterprises (SMEs), 7–19, 21–23, 26, 30, 33–41, 45–52, 56, 59–67, 71–75, 77, 79–83, 85–91, 94, 95, 98, 99, 108, 111–133, 135–145, 149–151, 153, 154, 157,

159–167, 170–178, 180–187, 189–201, 204–206, 210, 211, 219–226, 230, 231, 233–236, 238, 241–243, 245–247, 253–256, 258, 262–266, 268–270, 275–278, 281, 282, 284, 285, 290
Small Business, Enterprise and Employment (SBEE) Act 2015, 7, 263, 265
Small Business Innovation Research (SBIR), 181, 276, 283
Small Business Regulatory Enforcement Act of 1996 (SBREFA), 278
Small Enterprise Development (SEDA), 241, 248
SMB Development Strategy, 18, 219, 221, 225
SME Guarantee Fund, 171
SME parallel market (NOMU), 234, 236
SME Policy Grants, 12, 14, 191, 194
SME Productive Projects, 206, 210
SMEs Loan Guarantee Program (KAFALH), 233, 235, 236
SMEs Stimulus Comprehensive Plan, 38
social capital investment, 96
social entrepreneurship, 25, 28, 40, 146, 148, 243, 250
social fund, 82
social security payment, 138
socioeconomic, 166
South Africa, 14, 22, 27, 241–250, 286
South African Institute of Entrepreneurship (SAIE), 249
Spin-Off Lean Acceleration (SOLA), 67
Sporttech, 55
Springboard, 55

stamp duty, 86, 171, 173, 175, 255
Stanford Technology Ventures Program (STVP), 288
startup counseling, 202
Start Up India, 7, 153
start-up visa, 8
streamlining, 8
subcommittees, 280
super-and hyper-depreciation taxation system, 171, 174
sustainability, 2
Swinburne, 56
Swissnex, 68
Switzerland, 68
synchronized, 109

T
tariff, 163, 255
Tax Incentives for Innovation, 45, 49
tax relief, 10, 35, 171, 174, 241, 243, 263
technological innovation, 1, 3, 15, 16, 37, 95, 113, 173, 226, 230, 256
Technology Business Incubators (TBIs), 96, 155
Technology Innovation Fund (FIT), 172, 176
Technology Transfer Law (1981), 35
teleconferencing, 178
teleworking, 22, 23, 41, 99, 128, 132, 188, 238
Tencent, 102
term loans, 245
Thunderbird, 289
Turkey, 22, 253–257, 259–261
Turkey's Small and Medium Industry Development Organization (KOSGEB), 9, 21, 27, 253–255, 257–260

U

unified guarantee system, 222, 223
United Kingdom (UK), 10, 12,
  16–18, 22, 23, 148, 263–266,
  268, 269, 271, 273, 274
United Nations (UN), 68
United Nations Development
  Programme (UNDP), 43
upgrades, 38, 61, 154
Uruguay, 120
USA, 215

V

VC, 164
venture fund, 3, 235
VIC, 52
vocational training, 68, 72, 101, 115,
  238
VTB, 223

W

wholesale lending, 245
wholesaler, 274
Wildtuin, 250

WIMEN, 42
Witwatersrand, 250
Women Empowerment Fund, 242,
  246
women entrepreneurship, 123, 133,
  168, 216, 246, 280
Work-Study Dual System, 24, 192,
  202, 203
Wydler Technology, 277, 283

X

x-lab, 26, 81, 102

Y

youth entrepreneurship, 27, 28, 34,
  112, 125, 169, 172, 178, 202,
  215, 230, 242, 248, 250
youth unemployment, 28, 167, 242,
  244, 248–250
YouTube, 200

Z

Zuckerberg, 289

Printed in the United States
by Baker & Taylor Publisher Services

WIN OR LOSE

J. B. DUNCAN
Text by Jared Sams and Dale Jones

DARBY CREEK
MINNEAPOLIS

For all the coaches whose impact remains
long after they're gone.

Copyright © 2025 by Lerner Publishing Group, Inc.

All rights reserved. International copyright secured. No part of this book may
be reproduced, stored in a retrieval system, or transmitted in any form or by any
means—electronic, mechanical, photocopying, recording, or otherwise—without the
prior written permission of Lerner Publishing Group, Inc., except for the inclusion of
brief quotations in an acknowledged review.

Darby Creek™
An imprint of Lerner Publishing Group, Inc.
241 First Avenue North
Minneapolis, MN 55401 USA

For reading levels and more information, look up this title at
www.lernerbooks.com.

Main body text set in Janson Text LT Std.
Typeface provided by Adobe Systems.

Library of Congress Cataloging-in-Publication Data

Names: Duncan, J. B. (Children's author), author.
Title: Win or lose / J. B. Duncan; text by Jared Sams.
Description: Minneapolis : Darby Creek, 2025. | Series: Hoops Academy | Audience:
    Ages 11–18. | Audience: Grades 7–9. | Summary: When his basketball team keeps
    losing, Mojo seeks the help of his dad's former coach who teaches him valuable
    lessons about teamwork on a geocaching scavenger hunt.
Identifiers: LCCN 2024021413 (print) | LCCN 2024021414 (ebook) | ISBN
    9798765611395 (library binding) | ISBN 9798765661147 (paperback) | ISBN
    9798765651247 (epub)
Subjects: CYAC: Basketball—Fiction. | Teamwork (Sports)—Fiction. | Treasure hunt
    (Game)—Fiction. | LCGFT: Sports fiction. | Novels.
Classification: LCC PZ7.1.D847 Wi 2025 (print) | LCC PZ7.1.D847 (ebook) |
    DDC [Fic]—dc23

LC record available at https://lccn.loc.gov/2024021413
LC ebook record available at https://lccn.loc.gov/2024021414

Manufactured in the United States of America
1 – VP – 12/15/24

"Mojo, I'm open!"

I turn around at the sound of my name. George is standing off to the side, hands outstretched.

I hesitate, still dribbling the ball. George is fine on defense, but he can't catch the ball to save his life. I don't have to decide whether to pass to him, though, because right at that moment I see a flash of sea blue out of the corner of my eye.

I spin away as the other team's player reaches me, and his fingers *just* miss the ball.

"Mojo!" my other teammate Robin calls.

I pass him the ball, then dodge around the Kraken player and speed down the court toward the hoop.

"Watch number eight!" I hear the other coach yell and can't help but smile. That's my number.

I feel the Kraken player on my heels and glance up at the clock. Barely ten seconds left in the game, and we're down by ten points.

Robin passes back to George, but the ball is stolen. The Kraken player makes a break for it, and I change directions, dashing back toward our side of the court.

Our center Jason runs in one direction, and the Kraken player dodges to the side, easily getting around him. Their shoes squeak on the shiny wooden floor, and the crowd in the stands roars.

I block all of it out, focusing on my breathing and on where I'm headed. We might have lost this game, but we at least shouldn't let the other team score with less than five seconds left.

I make it to the other player just as he

jumps. The ball rolls off his fingers, and I launch myself into the air after it. My fingertips brush the rough orange surface, but it's not enough to knock it off course.

Swish! It's all net. The buzzer goes off right before the ball hits the floor, and the visitor side of the court erupts, screams and cheers echoing off the walls and floor.

I look up at the scoreboard. 52–65, Krakens. I grit my teeth. *Another* loss, the fourth in a row. We haven't won even once this season.

Coach Ty is gesturing for us all to gather around him at the sidelines.

I keep my head down as I head over. We should be better than this, especially since the whole point of going to Hoops Academy is basketball. The other teams at our school are the top in the state.

Four losses might not be such a big deal at another school, but at Hoops, it's shameful. It's embarrassing, especially as team captain, that our freshmen team can't win even once.

"Good hustle out there, guys," Coach Ty

says as we all walk off the court.

"You were so close on stopping that last shot, Cap! Great job!" George claps me on the shoulder, grinning. I try to give him a smile, but honestly, he's part of the problem. I don't think he's caught even one pass in any game this year.

"Thanks, George," I say, trying to sound sincere, but I don't know how successful I am. I hate losing. We're definitely not hustling. If we were, we'd be winning.

"All right, guys, let's meet in the locker room!" Coach says as we gather up our water bottles.

I follow him out of the gym, keeping my eyes off the stands. My parents are sitting there. They come to all my games. My father was a star player when he was at Hoops Academy, then went on to play in the NBA. There are a million trophies that have his name on them decorating the cases in the hallways, and everybody expects me to live up to his legacy. I'm Trey "Mojo" Michaels! I'm supposed to be a great basketball dynasty, but this team can't get a single "W" on the record.

In the locker room, everybody is chatting while Coach Ty stands in the middle of the locker room and claps to get our attention.

"All right, everyone," he says as we all turn to look. "I could see how hard all of you were working out there, and I know it's disappointing to lose. We need to work more on communication out there on the court. Talk to each other, and just as importantly, *listen*. We'll work on that in practice this week. Even with the loss, I've seen you boys improve this year, and I think we're on the right track." He turns to look at me. "Mojo, you were great out there. Awesome job scoring and keeping up with the other team. Think about what I said, though, and keep an eye out for everyone else—your teammates are there to help you."

I smile and nod, but the congratulations feel empty. Who cares if I played well? I always play well. It still doesn't mean that we won. My teammates are supposed to help me, but so far they haven't, and I can't pass to them if I know they're not going to catch it. We're already doing badly, and I'm the only one that I can depend on out on the court. Of course, I can't say any of that to Coach Ty.

"Thanks," I say. "I'm sure we can win the next game!" I'm *not* really sure, but Coach Ty at least seems convinced.

"Great attitude, Mojo. It's important to stand back up when you lose and see how you can improve. It's still just the start of the season, and we've got a bunch more games to come."

So far this year, Coach Ty hasn't taught me anything I don't already know.

I don't care that our thirteen-point loss was better than last week when we were twenty-one points down. Even if we've improved (slightly), it's still not enough to win, which is what's really important here.

At least my teammates seem to agree with me about that.

"I wish we could win even one game," George says, like he's not part of the problem. "It's frustrating to feel like everyone else is walking all over us all the time."

"Have you seen the way JV and varsity look at us?" Terry adds. "They don't respect us."

"They won't ever respect us if we can't even bring home a single freshmen team win," Robin says. "We practice so much. What's it going to take to finally get a win?"

Coach Ty speaks up, "Practice is the only way to improve. You boys have a nice weekend, and I'll see you all after school on Monday. Think about how you could improve over the weekend. We'll have a discussion first thing, then make a plan to improve."

Everybody turns back to their lockers, including me. I pop mine open and stare at the door.

At the start of the year, I taped a picture of the championship trophy to the inside as motivation. That's what I'm working for.

This year could help define my career at Hoops Academy. I'm the captain! How the team does reflects on me, and without a winning record, I worry that I won't have a chance of making varsity next year. If I can't do better than leading my team to a string of increasingly humiliating losses, I'll be bottom of the barrel and never get a chance to play for the rest of high school.

More than that, though, I want to *win*.

My parents are waiting for me outside the locker room talking to a large group of people I don't recognize.

This isn't uncommon; they both played pro for almost twenty years. They met at Hoops Academy and stayed together through their whole careers. Even though they're both retired now, they still get recognized and people stop them to ask for a selfie or an autograph.

I can't even manage to eke out a single high school victory. I hang back, waiting for them to finish.

Dad glances over at me, and I hitch up the strap of my gym bag uncomfortably. Now with him looking at me, embarrassment and guilt surround me like players on an opposing team. Except these, I don't know how to get around. They're just there, boxing me in. I should be better than this.

"Sorry, my son's here," Dad says, stepping back from his fan. Mom takes one last selfie with one of the girls, then shakes her hand.

Dad scoops me up in a big hug with Mom right behind him.

"Great job, buddy," she says, running a hand through my hair. I'm almost as tall as she is now, but she did that to me when I was little and never stopped. It reminds me of when I was learning to play basketball. Every time I made a basket, she'd do it.

"You played a great game," Dad says. "You almost stopped that last shot!"

He's been supportive all year and says he doesn't care if the team wins or loses. He's just glad I love the game as much as he does, but I feel bad anyway. I know he'd really love for me to win and bring home a championship for Hoops.

He won the championship every year he was at the school, and I always thought I'd do the same.

"Almost isn't good enough!" I say, stomping out of the building into the parking lot and toward our car.

"So, what do you think you did wrong?" Mom asks. She pops the trunk open and I put my gym bag inside. "How could you do better in the future?"

"I should have known Jason couldn't stop him and gotten started sooner," I say.

"Think about *you*, Mojo."

"I guess I could have, I dunno, jumped sooner? Run faster?" I'm already the fastest on the team by far.

"That's a good start. We can work on that this weekend if you want," Mom says, smiling at me.

We get in the car and my dad backs out. He waves out the window at the fans, who are standing around still staring at him and Mom.

I cross my arms and lean back so they can't see me.

Maybe I should transfer schools and join a different team. Not the Krakens, though. I need to go somewhere nobody's beaten me yet. It would be too embarrassing otherwise. No, I would need a fresh start where I can *really* start my basketball career.

"Coach Ty isn't pushing everybody hard enough," I burst out. "He doesn't *know* what it takes to win."

"Give him a break. It's his first year," Mom says. "He's trying to get his footing and still getting to know all of you and the school culture."

"I remember my coach when I was at Hoops Academy," Dad says before I get the chance to protest. "Coach Kit. He was the best."

We've all heard about Coach Kit, even the students whose parents weren't coached by him. He's the winningest coach in Hoops history, and he led the school to almost twenty championships. There's a big

12

picture of him in one of the display cases in the hallway, surrounded by ribbons and championship cups. Coach Kit is also part of the reason that Dad went into the NBA. He saw Dad's skill when he was just a freshman and took him under his wing.

I was expecting something like that to happen during my freshman year.

I expected that the coach would see how great I am and decide that he was going to nurture my talent, but Coach Ty didn't do that. I need my own Coach Kit.

"That man made us work for it!" Dad sounds wistful, like he usually does when he talks about his time at Hoops. "Every time we won a championship, he'd throw a big party at his house. All the school's teams were invited, and he'd barbecue food all day. It was packed, but we always had a blast."

"Sounds awesome," I mutter, trying not to sound resentful.

It *does* sound awesome, but it doesn't help me. My coach isn't Coach Kit. Coach Ty's just a newbie who doesn't understand what it takes to win.

I'm hit by a sudden idea. What if Coach Kit *was* my coach? He loved Hoops Academy and Hoops loved him. Surely he'd come out of retirement to help the team if he knew how much trouble we were in.

"What happened to Coach Kit?" I ask, trying to sound casual.

My parents exchange looks. "Well, he retired a while ago, and then after a couple of years, he sort of dropped off the map," Mom says.

"Why?"

"Nobody really knows," Mom says. "He was one of the most respected people in the city, but now he's become a recluse. Doesn't come out much, doesn't usually pick up the phone."

"It's a mystery," Dad adds. "Even I can't get through to him these days, and he and I were close for a long time."

I sit back again, staring out the window. Coach Ty can't be my Coach Kit, but he doesn't have to be. I can get someone even better. Who could be better than Coach Kit himself? He saw something in my dad, and I know he'll see that same thing in me.

3

The next morning, I sneak downstairs before my parents are up to look through Dad's contact book. He still keeps everything written down in a notebook on his desk, even though it's all in his phone now, too. It's old-fashioned, but so is he. I quickly skim the pages, looking for Coach Kit. Once I find him, I put the address into my phone. It's too far to walk, but I can take the bus.

I text my parents that I'm going out with George and Robin and sneak out before they can ask too many questions. The bus arrives at the stop a minute after I do, and I spend the whole ride thinking about how to approach Coach Kit.

If my dad is a basketball legend, then Coach Kit feels like a basketball myth. My parents say I met him when I was little, but I don't remember it, and he's never come around again as far as I can tell. Coaching stories about him float around our household, and Dad loves to repeat lessons that Coach Kit taught him. I don't really know anything else about him, though, and I wish I knew why he'd kept to himself and stopped showing up in public. I'm worried I might have trouble convincing him to come out of his house and help me. But he must love basketball since he coached for so long. Plus, once he knows who I am and sees that I have promise, I'm really hoping he'll agree.

Getting off the bus, I find Coach Kit's house is in a nice, upscale neighborhood. His house doesn't match the neighborhood at all. The paint on the siding is starting to peel, there are weeds growing up between the bricks of the path leading to the door, and I have to push aside a couple of low-hanging branches as I walk up the path. He must be home because there's a car in the driveway, but the curtains are pulled over the front windows and I don't see any lights on behind them.

At the bottom of the front porch steps, I pause and take a deep breath. Now that I'm here, I'm a little uncertain. My talents have always been with a basketball, not with words. Maybe I should have waited and asked one of my parents to come with me or at least gotten more information on Coach Kit before I came. For a moment, I think about turning around, but then the picture taped up in my locker springs to the front of my mind. I want to win. No, I *have* to win. This is the only way.

I knock on the door, ready to wait, but at my touch it swings open. The hallway beyond is dark and smells a little musty.

"Hello?" I call inside. There's no response. "Hello?" I repeat.

I look over my shoulder at the bright street behind me before stepping into the darkened hall. I leave the door open behind me, so there's enough light that I don't trip over anything. The doorway to my left leads to a large living room, with only a little light coming in around the edges of the curtain. When my eyes adjust, I can see that the walls are lined with shelves that are practically groaning under the weight of the trophies filling them.

I step forward and run my thumb over the plaque on one, picking up a layer of dust. *Hoops Academy, Championship 1986.* That was Dad's first championship year! I look at the next. It's for 1987. Pictures are tucked behind the trophies, and I'm just about to pull one of them out to take a closer look when I hear a loud voice coming from farther into the house. The words are indistinct, but whoever's saying them is *definitely* mad.

My heart jumps. I walk back into the hallway and look toward the sound of the voice. Then I glance at the door and the bright street beyond it. It's tempting to just go back out the door and head home, especially when I hear the voice again. No, our team has had too many losses already this year, and I can't let it continue, not if I can stop it. I'll just take a look down the hall. If Coach Kit seems too angry, I'll turn around and leave and come back tomorrow. I take a deep breath and creep farther down the hall, the voice getting louder as I get closer.

"We've been planning this for *months*!" the voice yells. "What do you mean, you can't make it work?"

I peer around a corner into a small kitchen, hoping not to be seen. A man sits at the table with his back to me, a phone pressed to his ear. His fingers grip it so tightly that his knuckles have turned white and bloodless. The other hand is curled into an equally tight fist on the table. The rest of his body is almost perfectly still, even as he shouts. Maybe this is a bad time.

"I can't *believe* you would do this—no, no. You made a promise!" He pauses, and his shoulders tense. "Fine. Then that's that." In a sudden burst of movement, he throws the phone down on the table and buries his head in his hands.

Yeah, it's time for me to leave. I turn to go, but a board creaks under my foot. The man's head whips around and I freeze. It's Coach Kit for sure. I recognize him from his pictures. He was a lot younger then, his face smooth and he had jet black hair. Now he has deep lines around his mouth and eyes, and his hair has turned to salt and pepper.

"Who are you?" he demands.

"I'm . . . Mojo," I stammer out. "Mojo Michaels. You knew my father—"

"Jay Michaels?" He suddenly looks less angry and more sad. "What do you want and why are you in my house, Mojo Michaels?"

"I—um—I came to ask for your help. With basketball."

Coach Kit turns all the way around and leans back casually, almost looking at me with dismissal. "I don't do that anymore."

"No, please!" I step forward into the kitchen, holding out my hands. "I'm at Hoops Academy, on the freshman team. We really, *really* need your help. We've lost every game so far this season. I need to win. Please come coach us!"

Coach Kit stands up and approaches me. He's nearly as tall as my dad. I stand still as he looks me up and down. I don't know what I'm going to do if he says no. "You'll do," he says. "Come with me."

"I'll do for what?" I ask, but Coach Kit has already stepped around me and is headed out toward the door. I scramble after him. "Coach Kit?"

He stops to grab his jacket and a small bag I hadn't noticed sitting by the front door.

"You've got a bus pass, right?" he asks, turning to me.

I take the card out of my pocket to show him. "Coach Kit, you haven't told me what we're doing."

"I'm doing a scavenger hunt today, but my partner dropped out. You're going to help me."

"Wait. What? No, no, no. Why would I do that? I came to ask for *your* help with basketball, not to help you with a scavenger hunt."

He ushers me out the door and pulls it closed behind him. "Because if you help me, then I'll help you."

I sigh, looking at him.

I don't want to spend my Saturday running around the city with my dad's old coach. On a basketball court with him, sure, where I might actually learn something useful, or show him how good I am. Then he'd decide to take me under his wing, just like he did with my father.

I need to convince him that I'm worth it, and the best way to do that is on a court.

"If you want help from me, surely you must be willing to help me in turn. You don't want my help, Mojo Michaels?"

I put up my hands in defeat. If this is the only way, I'll do it. "Fine. I'll help you. What do we have to do?"

"Perfect!" Coach Kit shoves the bag at me, and I sling it over my shoulder. "Let's go."

24

I follow him down the sidewalk and back onto the street, heading back to the bus stop I just came from. "Next bus is in . . . one minute! We'd better hurry."

Coach Kit takes off in a sprint down the sidewalk.

I follow him, my feet pounding on the pavement. He's surprisingly fast, and I only catch him at the corner.

"Just in time!" Coach Kit says as the number fourteen bus headed for downtown Spalding pulls up.

We find a couple of empty seats toward the back and sit down. Coach Kit pulls out his phone and opens an app, tilting the screen so I can see it.

"This is the scavenger hunt. Or the first part of it, at least," he says.

I glance down at the map. It's the central part of downtown, with a few locations marked on it with red pins. "What are those pins for?"

"Clue locations, of course! We have to find the clues and put them together in order to solve the scavenger hunt. Haven't you ever done a scavenger hunt before?"

"Maybe when I was a kid," I say. "A long time ago."

"It'll come back to you, I'm sure," Coach Kit says. "Have you done any geocaching before?"

I've heard of it, of course, and a bunch of kids at my school are into it. I tried it once with a couple of friends, but it wasn't really interesting to me. Running around looking for random notebooks to write my name in didn't feel like a great use of my time. "Sort of. A little."

If I sound annoyed, Coach Kit ignores it. He laughs loudly and some of the other people on the bus look around at us. "You're going to love it! Kids do this kind of stuff all the time."

"*You're* not a kid," I point out.

"Says who?" he asks, gesturing to himself with a big grin.

I try not to look *too* skeptical. "Ummm—" I can't say anything to offend him, but it's pretty obvious that he's not a kid anymore.

"Just playing with you, Mojo," he says after a long moment when it becomes clear I'm not going to say anything else. He jostles me good-naturedly with his elbow.

"I may look old to you, but I feel young on the inside." He snaps his fingers. "Someday you'll feel the same way, I'm sure, and today will feel like yesterday."

Coach Kit seems to notice that I didn't follow him entirely, because he moves on. "Ah, but enough of that. You're here for adventure, not for life lessons from an old-timer like me."

"Sure." It's not like I had much of a *choice* to come along if I want Coach Kit to help me. "What're we looking for on this scavenger hunt, anyway?"

"A treasure, unspeakably valuable," Coach Kit says, arcing his hand through the air and looking off above the heads of the other passengers like he can see something that's invisible to the rest of us.

"So it's like . . . money?" Spending time on a treasure hunt doesn't sound so bad if there is some cash at the end of it.

"No, of course not! Nothing so common as that." Coach Kit gives me a disapproving look. "I should think you'd know better."

I feel like I'm getting whiplash from all this back and forth, and I *still* have no idea what exactly it is that we're doing. "I don't—"

"Do you have this app?" Coach Kit asks, flashing his phone at me again. "You're going to need it for the scavenger hunt."

I actually do have it downloaded, from that time I geocached with my friends. I pull the app up on my phone.

Coach Kit helps me find the correct scavenger hunt game and adds me as a friend. A notification pops up that I've been added to Coach Kit's party and a pulsing green circle appears right next to my blue one.

"That's me," Coach Kit says, pointing to the green dot on my screen. "Now you can see where I am, and I can see where you are!"

"Why would I need that?"

"It's a partner game, of course!"

Before I can ask him what exactly he

means by that, he stands up, grinning.

"We're here! Off the bus, Mojo, and on to adventure!"

5

We get off the bus in a rush of people, and I'm almost swept away by the crowd before Coach Kit seizes me by the arm and pulls me toward a building.

"Don't go getting lost now, Mojo. That's for later." He peers at his phone, holding it close to his face. "Now let's find out where we're going."

I look at my own app, trying to figure out where the scavenger hunt starts. We're not in downtown proper where all the skyscrapers are, but these buildings are still pretty tall, and I'm not really familiar with this part of the city. It's mostly a shopping district, with stores and restaurants lining both sides of the street and apartments above. The sidewalks are full of people, walking fast and staring at their phones. The street is packed with cars, and the air smells of sweat, exhaust, and a little bit like freshly cooked French fries.

"This way!" Coach Kit says triumphantly, pointing to our left.

"Wait! I still don't know what we're doing!"

"There's a description in the app. Aren't you kids all over the apps these days? Don't you know how to find the information you need?"

I don't bother to point out that not only does that not make sense—what does *all over the apps* mean?—but also that I just found out about this minutes ago and haven't had a chance to even wrap my mind around what is going on. I thought we would just be practicing some expert drills or something so he could see how good I am.

"Can you just explain it to me, please?" I plead.

"This is a team scavenger hunt, which means that we need to work together. You'll be looking for one part, and I'll be looking for the other. We will each find clues that lead us to the other's next spot, so we need to stay in communication."

"Like with our phones? I can text you."

Coach Kit looks shocked. "Texting? No, I don't do that. Too impersonal. Give me my bag."

I hand it over and watch as he rummages around for a few moments. "Aha!" He pulls out an orange-and-black walkie-talkie and shoves it at me before going back in for the second.

"Walkie-talkies?" I turn the heavy device over in my hand. It feels like a brick against my palm. Wouldn't it be so much easier to just text?

"Indeed. Perfect for immediate communication. One button, no typing. Just the basics." He fiddles with his for a moment and a light on the top comes on, shining green.

"Perfect." Coach Kit hooks the walkie-talkie on his belt and pulls out his phone again.

"Now that we're all set, it's time to begin the hunt! Are you ready, young Mojo?"

"Sure," I say. I feel like I'm stepping onto a totally different playing field, like a soccer pitch or baseball field. There are rules to this game, but I don't know what they are, and I don't know any of the moves or skills. But if this is what it takes, I guess I'll figure out the rest of the game as we go along.

"What way did I say it was?" Coach Kit asks, looking around.

"That way." I point in the direction he'd indicated earlier.

"Excellent! Good to have another young mind around. Off we go!"

I follow Coach Kit into the crowd. It's late morning, so the lunch rush hasn't crowded the restaurants yet, but there's still a lot of people out shopping, and it takes a little bit of dodging to keep track of Coach Kit.

We come to the next corner and he consults his phone again for a moment before turning to cross. "It's the next street over, I think."

A man shoves by me carrying what seems like twenty shopping bags from upscale clothing stores, followed by a group of five or six girls around my age, chattering loudly. I press myself close to the wall as they pass, waiting until the sidewalk is clearer before I turn back to Coach Kit. He's staring intently at the map on his phone.

"All right, so it looks like one is on this side and the other's across the street. Which one do you want to take?"

"You mean we have to split up?" I ask.

"Of course! What did you think the walkie-talkies were for?"

"I guess just in case we got separated."

"Nonsense. We are *supposed* to be separated so we can work as a team. Get it?"

"Sure." I shrug. Only about half of what he says makes any sense to me, but I'm beginning to feel like that's just the way he talks.

"Great! You can take the other side. Better you stepping up and down those curbs than me, if I can help it. My knees aren't what they used to be." He winces and wrinkles his nose.

34

"Now do you have the map ready?"

I open the app on my phone and take a closer look. Sure enough, a pin has appeared on the other side of the street, about halfway up the block. "So, I'm just trying to find this location?"

Coach Kit nods seriously. "Yes, and then there will be a capsule hidden in that area. The capsule will have something inside with a code. When you enter the code on the app, I'll get the location of the next capsule. There will be another code in there . . . and so on. You get it."

It sounds easy enough. "All right. Let's get started."

It turns out that the treasure hunt is *not* easy enough. I find the spot pinned on the map, but there's nothing here; it's just a blank patch of sidewalk in front of an art supply store. I try not to walk into people as I turn in circles, staring at the ground for any hint of what I'm looking for.

The walkie-talkie in my pocket crackles. "How's it going over there, Mojo?"

"There's nothing here," I say, turning in a full circle, staring at the ground.

"And you're sure you're at the right spot?"

I double-check the map on my phone. My

blinking blue dot is directly underneath the pin on the map. "Yep, I'm sure. I can't find anything. Just sidewalk."

"Nope, you're missing something. Look some more."

"This might be easier if I knew what I was looking for," I say, trying hard not to sound irritated. "What does this capsule look like?"

"I don't know," Coach Kit says. "It could be anything. A box, or a bag. Maybe even an envelope."

"I don't see anything like that."

"Keep looking."

I pick up a couple of pieces of trash and throw them out, hoping that maybe the capsule got hidden underneath one of them, but it's just more dirty concrete. I feel like I'm starting to get weird looks from people passing me when the walkie-talkie crackles to life again.

"How'd it go, Mojo?" Coach Kit asks, then laughs a little. "Hey, that rhymes!"

"I swear, there's nothing here."

"Doesn't look that way to me."

"Excuse me?" I spin around, but he's nowhere near me. "How do you know where I am?"

"I can see across the street. Why don't you tell me what you see?"

"The sidewalk. The front of the store. Lots of people." I throw up my hands in frustration. "The planter box." It's got a sad-looking tree planted in it, dwarfed by all the buildings surrounding it.

"And you checked the planter box?"

"Of course."

"What about the tree?"

I pause. "I mean, I looked around the roots. But it's just dirt and some trash."

"For someone so tall, you're incredibly focused on the ground. If you only keep your eyes focused on your footwork, you'll miss the basket."

"You mean I should look in the actual tree?"

"I have imparted my wisdom. Now you can do with it what you will."

I tuck the walkie-talkie back into my

pocket and look more closely at the tree. It's not terribly tall, but I climb on the raised edge of the planter box to get a closer look anyway. At first, I don't see anything. I'm about to radio Coach Kit back and tell him that the tree is a no-go when I spot something unnaturally bright green tucked up in a branch. I reach up to grab it and realize it's a plastic jar, a little smaller than my hand. There's a label on the side that says *Spalding Geocache Scavenger Hunt 2025*. Inside is a folded piece of paper with just a set of numbers on it.

"Coach Kit, I've found it!" I call into the walkie-talkie.

"Great job, kid! I knew you could do it," he replies. "What's the code?" I read it out to him, then repeat it again when he misses a number the first time. "Got it!" he says triumphantly. "Now Mojo, put the clue back right where you found it. We can't ruin the game for everyone else."

"Wait, put it *back*?" I ask. "We found it. If we're going to win, then maybe we could move it somewhere else?" Putting it back feels like sitting our defense out and letting the other team take shots. That's no way to win a game!

"Mojo," Coach Kit's voice sounds sad. "That's not what this game is about."

"If we're racing for a treasure, though—"

He cuts me off. "There's more than one way to win, and you don't have to always play so aggressively. You have to remember, this isn't basketball anyway. Basketball is a competition, but geocaching is about playing the game. We don't want to ruin it for everybody else. That's not good sportsmanship, and you won't get far if you don't have that. Right now, your focus should be on playing the game, not on getting to the end. Think about that while I head off to find the next clue!"

I look down at the plastic jar in my hands. When I was a kid playing on neighborhood teams, sometimes my dad would ask me not to score, even when I was much better than the other team and could get past them easily. He said that it was bad sportsmanship to stop the other teams from playing just because we were so much better than them.

40

I didn't really understand it then, but now, after we've had opponents scoring against us all the time this year, I think I do. Not that I want anybody to go easy on us, but it sucks to feel like we're always being crushed, even if our team is worse than our opponents.

I carefully tuck the jar back between the branches, then take a critical look at it. I can see it, but not everybody is as tall as I am. I step back up and move it slightly so it's a little more visible. Easier for the next person, and maybe they won't waste so much time looking on the ground for it.

I sit on the edge of the planter and wait for Coach Kit to radio me. After about a minute of silence, I radio him instead.

"Coach Kit? How's it going?"

It takes a couple seconds for him to respond. "Lots of people 'round these parts. Hard to get a good look. Plus, my eyes aren't what they used to be."

"I can come help," I offer. Maybe it will go faster that way.

"No need for that. I'll find it."

After a few more minutes of waiting in silence, I radio him again. "Any update?"

"Almost got it, kid. No need to be so impatient." He sounds out of breath, like he's been running or something.

"Are you sure you don't want my help?" I'm getting a little frustrated with him, though I'm doing my best to conceal it. He was impatient about me searching for my clue but doesn't want me to help him? Coach Kit said this was supposed to be a group activity, but we're not even together.

I jiggle my feet, uncomfortable sitting still. It's like sitting on a bench, watching my teammates play without me.

I'm ready for the coach to put me in, but Coach Kit is keeping me out. So far, none of this is improving my basketball skills. He said he'd help me when we were done, but he won't let me help him finish, so I'm trapped in this limbo.

It's starting to get hot, and the concrete sidewalk radiates heat up from underneath me, even in the shade. Honestly, I'm not sure I'll stay for much longer if Coach Kit continues like this. I'm not sure *any* basketball coaching is worth it.

Dad had said that Coach Kit became a recluse, and for the first time I'm starting to seriously think that it was for a good reason. Maybe he's trying to put me off because his basketball skills are rusty and can't really help me.

Or, it strikes me, he might not even *understand* what I want. So much of what he says doesn't make sense. This man doesn't match at all what Dad described to me in the past, either as his coach and mentor, or what he said in the car the other night.

After what feels like forever, the radio crackles with Coach Kit's voice. "I found it! Okay Mojo, here's my clue. Clark and Orange. Does that mean anything to you?"

I examine the map on my phone, looking for an intersection that matches those two, and find it not too far from us. Clark and Orange are both big streets, and an enormous park takes up almost a whole block on one corner.

There's a bus line that goes straight there as well, so we can even get out of the heat for a minute. "Got it."

We ride the bus over to the next location and get off across the street from a big park on the corner of Orange and Clark.

Coach Kit squints at his phone. I've never been to this park before, though it's got a basketball court. There's also a playground with a picnic area and a few fields where people have set up nets and are playing soccer.

Right in the middle is a set of attached buildings with the words *Community Center* on the side. I take a look at the map on my screen and see a new pin has appeared across the street from our two blinking dots.

"Great. Let's go," I say.

The pin is dropped in the center building. I hold the door open for Coach Kit and follow him in, taking a look around.

The linoleum floor is clean but clearly old and well-used, and in front of us is a wide desk with an employee standing behind it.

The employee smiles at us when we come in. "How can I help you today?"

"We're looking for—" I begin to explain, but Coach Kit cuts me off.

"Now, now, we can't ask her for help. We have to find it ourselves."

She gives us a knowing look. "I get it. You're doing the scavenger hunt."

"Yes. Get a lot of folks coming through?" Coach Kit asks.

"Oh yeah. In fact, there was another team here just fifteen minutes ago."

"We're right on their heels, Mojo!" Coach Kit does a little shooing gesture toward me. "You start over there." He gestures to a bunch of brochures in a rack on the wall, along with a small bookshelf, then turns to take the other side of the room.

I resist rolling my eyes as I go over to the rack of brochures. They're all for programs offered by the community center.

I don't pay too much attention to them since none of them have a little green jar shoved behind.

Instead, my eye is caught by the basketball court I can see through the window, and the group of people playing a pickup game. Some of them are quite good, and one girl is just jumping to shoot when I hear Coach Kit calling my name. My concentration breaks and I turn back to him.

"Anything over there?" he asks. His tone makes it clear that he knows I got distracted and wasn't really looking for the capsule.

I give the rack a final halfhearted once-over before saying, "Not over here."

Across the room is a large diorama about the history of the city, but we don't find the capsule there either.

Coach Kit spends a long time looking at

a tiny construction crane on the diorama and reading the descriptions posted above it.

The longer he takes, the more frustrated I become. I feel it all building up like a basketball-sized knot in my chest, and it makes me want to scream.

After what feels like five hours, he finishes reading the last description on the diorama and looks up at me.

"No capsule here. Not even a miniature one to match the diorama!" He smiles wide at his joke, but I can't make myself smile back. It takes all my self-control not to snap at him when I speak.

"Maybe we're in the wrong place?"

"No, no." Coach Kit rubs his chin thoughtfully. "This is where the pin is on the map. But we're missing something . . ." His eyes catch on the employee podium. "Excuse me, Miss, but you mind if I took a look at your podium?"

The employee steps back. "Go right ahead."

He barely looks for five seconds before

he bends down with a loud, "Aha!" When he stands up, he's holding another green plastic jar.

I pull out my phone and input the numbers as he reads them to me. A pin pops up across the park. "It's here. Let's go."

Coach Kit puts the jar back on the podium as I head out the door. I hear Coach Kit say goodbye to the employee before following me out.

"Mojo, you don't seem like you're having fun," Coach Kit says as he comes up beside me.

"Should I be having fun?" I ask, then realize how snappy that sounds. "I mean, this just isn't what I expected to spend my Saturday doing, is all."

"Sometimes the unexpected things are the best, though," Coach Kit says. "Haven't you ever had an opponent do something on a court that you didn't see coming, that you couldn't even imagine someone doing? Then you get the chance to learn from it, pick up a new skill and a new perspective you hadn't even thought of before."

I stop, spreading my hands wide.

The basketball in my chest is getting bigger, like someone just keeps pumping air into it.

"But *this* isn't a new basketball skill. Nothing here is helping me become a better player. The only thing is that you want to do it, and I want your help."

"Skills can come from anywhere, Mojo, even from something that seems totally unrelated. Maybe the next time you're on a court, you'll think about the first capsule and look high instead of low. Or maybe your opponents will expect you to look in the obvious places for a teammate, and you'll remember the capsule here and go in a completely different direction."

"What?" I can't believe what he's saying.

I fully intend to never think about this scavenger hunt again if I don't have to, and I'm dying to get back on a court and do something *real*.

Coach Kit frowns at me. "I thought

that was what you wanted, to start winning. Wasn't that what you were telling me this morning?"

"Yeah, but I want to win at basketball, using *actual* basketball skills. What does any of this have to do with playing ball?"

It feels good to finally let go of my self-control and voice my frustration, the knot starting to loosen and shrink.

Coach Kit frowns. "It's not really about what this has to do with basketball, though, is it? It's about you. Winning is all in the attitude, and I can tell you right now, I do not see that winning attitude in you."

That shuts me up. For the first time all day, he sounds serious, and he's looking at me with genuine disappointment.

I've always thought of myself as a winner, despite the team's season record that obviously doesn't support that.

"I don't—I didn't—" I stutter, trying to protest even though I know he's right.

"You don't think that this matters. Maybe in the long run, it doesn't. But how you're approaching this game, right here right now, shows who you are, and *that* matters."

I glance at him, and the obvious disappointment in his eyes feels like every lost game rolled into one.

I scuff my shoe on the ground, too ashamed to look back at Coach Kit. The basketball-sized knot is back in my chest, bigger than before if that's even possible. "I'm sorry," I mutter. "That's not how I am, usually." It's definitely not how I want to be, at least.

I feel a heavy hand on my shoulder and look up. Coach Kit's eyes are kind and earnest, and that almost makes me feel worse.

"Mojo, it's okay. Today started out a little rough. I don't think either of us would deny that. Not every shot can be a slam dunk. Not all of them even make it through the hoop, but you should look at every missed shot as an opportunity for improvement, not a sign of failure."

I nod, swallowing hard. I wish I hadn't yelled at him and regret letting go of my control.

He's giving me another chance, and I'm not going to waste it. "Sounds good, Coach."

The pin is dropped in the playground, right in the center of the wooden play structure. A few kids are screaming and chasing each other around, but there aren't too many of them in the area. The structure is in a circle of wood chips, surrounded by a concrete sidewalk lined with benches and trash cans. The whole space is shaded by wide trees planted behind the benches.

"Do you think it's . . . in the actual play structure?" I ask, glancing over at Coach Kit.

"I guess we'd better check and see!"

We have to bend all the way down to check

the ground underneath the structure, and Coach Kit is undeterred when we come up empty on our first pass.

"Let's check up top!" he says cheerfully.

Fortunately, the structure doesn't have a roof, so we only have to duck to get under crossbeams and can stand the rest of the time. The structure is huge, with two sections and a bridge between them, so we start at one end and work our way across. As I'm crossing the bridge, I glance up and spot a now familiar flash of green.

"Coach Kit!" I call, pointing.

"Great job spotting that!" he says.

The jar is on top of the tallest pole in the structure, above both of our heads. Though we both try, neither of us can reach far enough to grab it. It doesn't even move when our fingertips brush it, so there must be something holding it in place.

"Should I just climb up and get it?" I say, looking quizzically at Coach Kit.

"Don't know what else to do. Be careful, though."

I put my foot on one of the railings and grab the crossbeam to lift myself up. From that height, I can see that the jar has been wedged into the center of the pole where it's rotted out, probably so it won't fall and get lost. I take it out and pass it to Coach Kit before stepping back down to join him again. He's already got it open, and on it is another code for the next capsule. The pin appears in the picnic area by the basketball courts.

"Wonderful!" Coach Kit says. "Not too far to walk, and maybe I can sit down a little bit."

"Sounds good!" Showing a winning attitude when you don't feel it is hard, so I try to make the words sound as genuine as possible in the hopes that I'll start to feel them, too, instead of just feeling frustrated and bored. I tuck the capsule back into the log, and when I come down, Coach Kit is staring at the slide.

"It's been years since I was on a slide. Decades, even. Why are slides just for kids? Shouldn't adults have fun, too?"

"Well, why don't we take the slide down?" It's been a long time since I was on a slide, too.

Coach Kit gestures for me to go first, so I sit down at the top. I have to lean almost all the way back so my head doesn't hit the crossbar on the top. It's a short slide, but I'm still a little exhilarated when I get to the bottom. Maybe Coach Kit has a point about slides for adults.

I step out of the way and hear Coach Kit whoop as he comes down after me. Some of the kids are looking at us—and some of the parents, too—but I don't care and neither does Coach Kit, by the way he stands up with a big goofy grin on his face.

"That's what life is about, Mojo! The fun! Now let's go have some more of it."

About half of the picnic tables are occupied by people, so we check all the empty ones first. The area is shady, but none of the tree branches are within easy reaching distance, so Coach Kit says the capsule probably won't be up there.

"They're not supposed to be impossible to find," he explains. "It's about getting out of your house and interacting with the world, even if interacting is just looking for little capsules other people have hidden."

That doesn't fit with what Dad told me about him becoming a recluse. In fact, Coach

Kit has been nothing like what I expected. I thought I'd have to do some convincing to get him out of the house and coach me since he'd locked himself away for so long. That hasn't been the case at all, though. If anything, he's *more* excited than I am to be out running around the city.

"It'll probably be in a joint under one of the tables," Coach Kit says, so I get started looking at each of the tables one by one. Of course, it takes until the second-to-last table to find the capsule, tucked right where Coach Kit said it would be in the corner of a joint.

I sit next to Coach Kit as I open it up and pull out the piece of paper. Just like before, the code pops up a new pin, this one all the way across the city. I crouch down to put the capsule back, and when I crawl out from under the table, Coach Kit is staring at the nearby basketball court. The pickup game I saw earlier just finished, and they leave the ball on a rack right by the hoop as they walk off, all joking and slapping each other's shoulders.

When Coach Kit looks back at me, there's a

new glint in his eye. "Let's unwind a little bit," he says, starting toward the court. I scramble to my feet and follow after. Finally, we're getting to some basketball! Now is the moment for me to show Coach Kit how good I am and to get some of the wisdom that he gave to my dad. Maybe I'll ask him for some help with my hook shot. I've been practicing and my mom's been teaching me, but I just can't get the angles right. Then I'll explain the mistakes that my teammates are making and how I'm trying to work around them. That way, Coach Kit can start making a plan for when he comes in to help us, and my teammates can start improving right away.

He grabs the basketball off the rack and tosses it at me. I barely get my hands up in time to stop it from slamming into my rib cage.

"You wanna play?" I ask, a little skeptical.

"I've still got the moves," he says, bouncing back and forth on his feet like he's ready to run. "C'mon, you don't think you can beat me?"

I can't let a challenge like that slide. "Oh, you're on." I drop the ball to the asphalt and start dribbling across the court toward the hoop. Coach Kit dodges in front of me, reaching for the ball. I spin to the side, thinking I've avoided him, but when I look back, the ball is in his hands now. I have no idea how he did that.

"Didn't see that coming, did you?" He gives me a playful grin and a wink.

"Okay, okay, I'll admit you are faster than I was expecting." This time when I go after the ball, I'm a little better prepared, but Coach Kit still avoids me. He moves so smoothly it's like water slipping between my fingers. The ball almost seems like it's part of his hand. If he plays this well now, I can't imagine what he was like back when he was coaching Dad. Coach Kit stops dribbling and shoots, the ball going straight through the hoop. If it had a net, it would have made that wonderful *swish* sound.

"Your turn," he says, and we trade places. The first shot I try, Coach Kit snatches it out of the air like it's nothing. The next time, I throw it a little higher. He has to jump to grab it, but he does catch it. Of course, he makes every shot perfectly.

Sometimes he'll stop play to give me a bit of advice. He has me shift my stance a little for my hook shot, and it actually seems to work. This is what I wanted from him to begin with, and it's even better than I could have hoped.

I have no idea how long we've been playing when I finally make a basket against his defense. I pump my fist in the air and give myself a little victory dance and cheer.

"Good game, Mojo," Coach Kit says, coming over to give me a fist bump. "You seemed like you were having fun."

"That was awesome! We're definitely gonna start winning if you teach everybody else on the team to play like that."

"All players have different strengths, Mojo. You're exceptionally good at shooting, and someone else might be perfect for defense. Not everybody on a team has to play the same way."

"Yeah, no, I understand that," I say. "I mean, to play at that level, no matter where on the court they are."

"We'll just have to see. For now, let's get

back to our adventure!" He tosses the ball to me and I replace it on the rack. I'd hoped he could help us earlier, but now I know for sure. No offense to Coach Ty, but this is what we need. With Coach Kit coaching us, we'll definitely start winning.

10

We take another bus across town to the final location in front of the Spalding Stadium, a big multipurpose arena surrounded by plazas and gardens. The pin doesn't take us inside the actual arena, though, which is good since it's locked up when there's no game going on. Instead, the pin is dropped in one of the garden areas off to one side. We're standing around peering at the app and trying to figure out where we're going when a group of people walk by, laughing and talking loudly. Coach Kit's head shoots up.

"Vern?" he asks, sounding astonished.

One of the men in the group stops, looking around. When his eyes land on Coach Kit, he freezes for a moment. He shifts on the balls of his feet as he looks at Coach Kit, like he's nervous.

"Kit, hi."

Coach Kit's jaw drops. "I thought you said you couldn't make it today."

Vern looks around at his friends. "I'll meet up with you all in a minute, if that's okay?" They all nod and head off.

"Vern?" Coach Kit sounds confused.

"Look, Kit, I'm sorry," Vern says, stepping closer. "I didn't mean . . . I just—"

"Didn't want to do it with me." Coach Kit's shoulders slump, his hands dropping to his sides.

"No, it's not that! I mean, I wanted to, but these guys asked, and the only day they were free was today. I thought maybe we could do the scavenger hunt together next weekend." Vern looks pleadingly at Coach Kit.

I'm still behind him, so I can't see his expression, but I can tell just from the way he's standing that he's especially upset.

"I could have gone with you," Coach Kit says quietly. His voice is small and hurt.

"I thought you probably wouldn't like these guys. I mean, they're . . . anyway, I didn't think you'd come out and do the hunt today, or I would have . . ." Vern trails off, lost for words. "But hey, it looks like you found someone to do the scavenger hunt with today. That's fun." Vern gestures to me, clearly trying to bring the mood back up. It's a totally transparent play, no subtlety at all.

"Uh, yeah. This is my . . . this is Mojo."

I step up beside Coach Kit, standing shoulder to shoulder with him, trying to give off an air of solidarity. My heart hurts for him, and I wish I could help somehow.

"Well, I guess I'll let you guys get back to it," Vern says. "It was nice to see you, Kit. Good to meet you, Mojo."

As soon as he's far enough away, I turn to Coach Kit. His face is all crumpled up, and he's staring blankly at the ground.

"Hey, Coach," I say gently. "Do you want

to sit down?" I guide him over to a nearby bench, and he lets me just move him along limply. It seems like all the life and joy has gone out of his body.

"We were supposed to do the hunt together today. We'd planned it for months. Then this morning he called and said he couldn't make it today. Didn't give me an explanation," he says.

"I heard the end of that conversation, I think," I say. "I'm so sorry, Coach Kit."

"I thought Vern and I were a team. We've known each other for twenty years at least."

I'm quiet for a moment, trying to think of something to say that might help him feel better. "When I was seven, I was on a basketball team, for a kid's league. The coach for the team was fine, but he was teaching the team stuff that my parents had shown me already. I got bored, and I didn't really get along with my teammates. One day, the coach gave one of my teammates bad advice. I don't even remember what it was about, but I jumped in and told the coach he was wrong. I showed the other player how my mom had taught me to do it. The other kids started asking me for help."

Coach Kit is looking at me, his face serious and attentive. "Did you help them?" he asks gently.

"Yeah. I finally felt like I was fitting in a little more. I mean, I loved basketball! It was what I'd grown up with, and I wanted to share everything I knew. I thought all the other kids were listening to me and liked me. Then one day, I was late to practice. When I got there, all the kids and the coach were talking. One of the kids, a boy I thought I was really friends with, said out loud that he hoped I wasn't coming because I was a know-it-all and he was tired of me acting like I was so much better than everyone." I break off and take a deep breath, staring at the ground.

Coach Kit puts a warm hand on my shoulder and squeezes gently.

I shake my head. The story isn't over. "All of the other kids started to agree with him. The coach did, too. My parents said I couldn't quit just because I'd met some mean kids, but they did let me switch teams instead. The new team turned out to be better." I pause, unsure of the story now that I've told it. I didn't want it to seem like I was trying to make Coach Kit feel bad for me and forget his story. "It's not exactly the same as your story, but I guess my point is that sometimes your first team sucks and you need to find a new one." It feels like a weak ending, but Coach Kit is nodding.

"That's a terrible thing for children to do, but worse for the coach. I'm sorry that happened to you."

"And I'm sorry that Vern bailed on you today," I say, trying to bring it back around to him. "We can't let that jerk ruin our day, though."

"No we can't," Coach Kit says. I can see a little bit of the old Coach Kit coming back. His eyes are starting to have that gleam of playfulness, and his shoulders aren't so slumped anymore. He sits up straight and looks around. "Now where were we?"

"We were headed into the garden. That's

where the pin is." I'm glad he didn't ask me more about the team. I don't want to think about that memory any longer than I have to.

He jumps to his feet. "Right then. Off we go!"

Large trees cast shade over winding dirt paths, and in the middle of the garden is an enormous water feature. Two waterfalls cascade down either side of a little cliff face and come together at the bottom to form a large pond. In the middle of the pond sits an island, covered in greenery and ferns.

We hunt around the garden, looking under all the bushes and around the edges of rocks, but there are no green capsules to be found. I'm rechecking around the base of a particularly leafy plant when I hear Coach Kit let out a big laugh. "Mojo, I found it!" he calls.

I come around the corner, expecting to see him holding the capsule, but instead, he's staring across at the little island in the center of the artificial pond.

"Where is it?" I ask.

He raises his hand to point, and that's when I see it. The capsule is sitting at the base of one of the plants on the island, clearly visible, but also clearly out of reach.

"How are we supposed to get to it?" I ask, astonished. "I thought you said they were supposed to be easy to find!"

"You can't say it's not easy to find," Coach Kit points out. "Look, it's right there where anyone can see it! So clever."

I eye up the river, trying to judge how wide it is. "Maybe I can jump it?" I say, but without much confidence. It's kind of a ways, even for someone tall like me.

"Nonsense, the rocks are slippery over there, even if you could make it," Coach Kit says. "There must be another way."

We walk all the way around the water, but the whole thing is wet on the edges and too wide to leap across.

"I can't see a way to get there. Did people just wade through the water?" I really, *really* don't want to have to do that. Who knows what's in there?

"No, I don't see any wet footprints," Coach Kit says, looking around at the ground. He freezes. "Oh, now that's clever."

"What is?" I ask, scanning the ground.

"It's the log. See how it's been recently moved." There's a log on the ground right by his feet, against the outer edge of the pond's rocky edge. The dirt around it is disturbed, and the log itself doesn't look especially dirty. "It's a bridge," he says.

Together we maneuver it so it crosses the water. The log is mostly flat on the ends, but the rocks are not so it wobbles when we put any weight on it. No matter which way we turn it, we can't get it to sit flat.

"I'll just have to try it," I say after we've been at it for five minutes. "Even if it means I might fall in."

Coach Kit is looking thoughtfully at the

log, then at the capsule, sitting just out of reach like it's teasing us. "This is supposed to be a team game," he explains. He puts both hands on the end of the log and presses down on it. "Try it now."

I reach over and shove the log as hard as I can, but it doesn't move. "Are you sure you can hold it still even when I'm standing on it?"

"Of course I can," Coach Kit says with a laugh. He puts a hand on my shoulder. "Mojo, I trust you to do your part. Can you trust me to do mine?"

I nod, swallowing down my worry. I don't think Coach Kit would ask me to do something he thought I couldn't do. I *do* trust him. "Yeah."

"Good man." He repositions his hands on the log. "I've got it."

I put one foot on it nervously, then the other. The log doesn't move. Another cautious step takes me out over the water. It suddenly seems like it's moving a lot faster now that I'm standing right above it. I close my eyes for a moment and imagine I'm on a court. The sound of the water is actually just people cheering in the stands, and the wood I'm standing on is painted with white lines. I just need to follow it, like it's some sort of footwork drill. The next step is much easier, and before I know it, I'm stepping onto the solid land of the island.

"You good?" Coach Kit asks, and I give him a thumbs-up.

I open the capsule quickly and pull out the slip of paper. Coach Kit types the code into his phone as I shout each number over. The pin drops in a plaza on the other side of Spalding Stadium. When we get there, we see the plaza is paved, and in the middle is a large bronze statue with a base surrounded by decorative stones. We search for twenty minutes and come up with nothing.

Coach Kit sits down on a bench, looking defeated. We've looked everywhere. Underneath all the bushes and benches, around the trash cans. He even had me climb onto the statue to see if it was hidden up high, like the one in the play structure. But no luck.

"I can't think of where else it would be," he says, looking sadly at the app. Our two pulsing dots are directly underneath the pin.

I'm not sure what else to say. It sucks that we can't find the last capsule after spending so much time and effort to hunt it down.

"We don't *have* to finish it," I finally manage. "We still had an adventure, right?" It sounds like something he would say to me, so I hope it helps him to feel better now.

"I guess you're right. We should look on the positive side here." He still sounds disappointed, though.

We lapse back into silence, and my gaze slides over the pile of stones around the bottom of the statue. Most of them are almost identical, arranged in neat rows, but one looks slightly out of place. I have a sudden idea.

"Hey Coach," I say, nudging him with my elbow. "You see anything weird about those rocks?"

He squints at them, then stands up to get a closer look. "You're right. One of them is not in the right place."

Together we crouch down by the statue and lift the out-of-place stone up. It's not heavy at all, because it turns out to be made of plastic and it is hollow on the inside. Underneath it is the last capsule. The final capsule is bigger than the previous ones but the same color green. Coach Kit takes it out with a look of absolute joy on his face.

"We did it! We finished the hunt!" he exclaims.

"Open it!" I say encouragingly. I want to see what the treasure is!

He puts one hand on the lid. "Here goes." He reaches inside slowly, and when his hand comes out, it's in a fist, holding something. "Are you ready?"

"Heck yeah!"

I know he's trying to draw out the excitement and make it seem suspenseful because he's moving so slowly. It's kind of working. He said it wasn't money, but something better. Maybe it's something that will help me with basketball! He did ask me to do this scavenger hunt with him after he knew I wanted help with the team. Maybe the whole thing has been some sort of build up to this, the answer to all of my team's problems. After what feels like forever, Coach Kit finally uncurls his fingers.

In the middle of Coach Kit's palm is a little troll doll. The paint is chipped and fading from its face, and its hair is dirty and tangled. It looks like it used to belong to a kid, then got left outside for a bit too long before being put in the capsule.

"That's it?" I ask. I can't believe what I'm looking at. After all this searching, we end up with a kid's toy?

"Yep!" Coach Kit sounds delighted. He quickly snaps a picture of the doll, then posts it to the app to record that he finished the scavenger hunt.

I look between the troll and Coach Kit in increasing astonishment. "That can't be it! You said that there was a treasure at the end."

"Did I?"

"Yes, on the bus," I remind him. "You said it was super valuable. That is *not* what I would define as a treasure." I thought a treasure would be something actually valuable or meaningful, if not a physical item, then at least knowledge. A new basketball skill, or something. Instead, I wasted all day chasing after an ugly doll.

"Mojo, a treasure is what you make of it. When you play basketball, the win comes at the end. It's not the game, it's not the plays, it's just where you want to go. What matters more is how you play the game, the decisions you make on the court. That's the real treasure. It's not what's at the end of the journey, it's what's in the middle."

I resist the urge to roll my eyes. That wasn't what I was asking back on the bus, and he must have known that. Now he's coming up with these cliches about the important part being the journey, not the destination. I've heard that before, and I'm not convinced it actually means anything.

"Why even bother doing this?" I demand.

Coach Kit looks down at the doll and the notebook. He seems a little hesitant when he speaks. "Mojo, I wasn't entirely truthful with you earlier."

"I don't understand," I say, confused.

He sighs sadly, staring down at the troll still in his hand. "After my wife died a couple years ago, I shut myself away. I stopped going out or seeing friends and just stayed hidden from the world. Then about a month ago, I started feeling ill. When I went to the doctor, he said . . ." He trails off, his voice breaking. I give him a moment as he takes a deep breath so he can continue. "Well, he said I might not have that much time left. Since that day, all I can think about are the things I didn't do and didn't see, even things that were right here in my home city under my nose the whole time. I heard about this scavenger hunt thing and thought that it would be a good chance for me

81

to get out of the house, or maybe just remind me how to be alive, put me back in the world a little bit."

I swallow hard. Coach Kit is sick? He seems so full of life and exuberant. I never would have guessed.

"Oh." I think I get it, but I'm not sure.

Coach Kit must see that I don't understand, so he leans back and looks at me thoughtfully. "Think about when you're playing and you make the perfect throw. The ball rolls off your fingers just right, and it traces the arc that only you can see in the air, the one you drew in your mind when you set up the shot. The first time you make it, it feels like magic. So you do it again, and you practice, and then you can do it every time."

He pauses and looks at me. I picture the court and the basket in my mind, but not the one in the school gym, or even the one in the park. It's the court in my backyard, where I learned to play. I'm five and for the first time, the ball goes right where I meant for it to. That's the moment I think I really fell in love with basketball. I knew I wanted to do that again, just like my mom and dad knew when they were kids. I felt it, deep inside. It's been years since I thought about that day.

"Now you can do it without even a thought, and the moment passes right by you. The magic isn't gone. It's just overlooked. Every perfect shot gives you the chance to experience that again, to bring the perfection in your mind into the world, right in front of you. That's what I was trying to find with this. That feeling, that little magic, was missing from my life," he says

I nod. I think I actually do understand what he means. "Coach Kit?" I hesitate, a little unsure of how to word what I'm feeling. "I'm . . . I'm sorry. About you, you know. Being sick." The words feel awkward and clunky, and not like they fully capture the truth of what I'm trying to say.

"Thanks, Mojo," he says with a small smile. "In a way, I'm grateful for the diagnosis. It pulled me out of my funk, and now I've done something I wanted to do. A bunch of things I wanted to do, actually. I couldn't really say that I was living before, locked away all alone in my house. Now, though, doing this. *This* is what life is about."

I feel even more at a loss for words. "Do you want to write our names in the book to show that we completed the scavenger hunt?" I offer.

"Absolutely!" Coach Kit replaces the doll in the capsule and opens the notebook. It's got a long list of names with dates next to them, and some doodles people took the time to draw. We add our names at the bottom of the last page, right underneath Vern's. I try not to get too irritated with him again.

"I guess we're all done," Coach Kit says. He seems a little sad.

I don't want to break the moment, but now that we've finished, I need to know. "Coach Kit? Can we talk about basketball now? You said you'd help me."

"The energy of youth. Can't let one adventure settle in before you're on to another."

"I just . . . our next game is coming up this

week," I say by way of explanation. We need to get started soon if the team is ever going to make progress.

13

"Let's talk training," he says, grabbing a basketball off a patio chair and tossing it to me now that we are on his personal backyard half court. It's not at all what I'm expecting. Instead of shooting or dodging, he has me practice passing. I pass him the ball when he's behind me, then in front, then to the side. I put it by his knees and his hands, his left shoulder, then his right.

"What is the point of this?" I ask after we've been doing this for half an hour, grabbing the ball and standing still, panting. It's not like I'd ever intentionally put a pass specifically by someone's left shoulder.

"That sounds like a complaint," Coach Kit says.

"I just want to know why you're having me practice this over and over again, and it might help me if I understood."

Coach Kit raises an eyebrow. "Think about it, Mojo. What are you learning?"

I shrug, getting irritated again. "I don't know! That's why I asked. I can do all of these things already."

I see that same look of disapproval in his eyes as he had at the park, when he confronted me about my attitude. This time, I have no idea what he wants from me, and we haven't talked about coaching the team at all. That was the whole point of today!

"All right, let's do something different." Just like at the park, he has me try to score against him, except this time, right as I'm about to shoot, he says, "Pass it to your teammate!" and points.

"What?" I pause, confused. There's nobody there, and I have a clean shot, so why would I pass? Coach Kit steals the ball right out of my hands.

"Hey, I was just about to score!" I say.

Coach Kit tosses the ball back to me. "Is the game actually about scoring, Mojo?"

"Of course! That's the whole point. Why would I throw the ball into empty space when there's just the two of us here?" I throw my hands up. "I don't get it!"

Coach Kit dribbles the ball slowly, eyes tracking each bounce. "Well, I'd seen you play before today."

"What? I've never seen you at the games." I try to think back, to see if I remember him in some corner of my mind. I'm pretty sure if he'd come, Dad would have noticed him and mentioned it, maybe even introduced us. But that never happened.

"The school streams all the games online, even the freshman ones. I still watch all of them, so I've seen you play this year." Coach Kit stops dribbling and looks straight at me. I feel an aura of seriousness descend over us, like he's about to say something really important.

"Look, Mojo. You're quite talented. I saw it today at the park, and I've seen it in every game I've watched you play. You remind me a lot of your dad at your age, actually."

"Really?"

"You've got an instinct for the game, for how to move the ball and how to play the court. I think you could go far, if pro basketball is what you're aiming for." He tosses me the ball; it's warm and familiar under my hands. Finally! This is what I've wanted to hear all day.

I'm unable to repress my grin. "Thanks, Coach."

"You've also got his flaws," Coach Kit continues, and I stop grinning. "Your dad was the best player on the team, too. He could do anything with the ball, like magic. But basketball is a *team* sport. You can't win it on your own. It took your dad a while until he learned that it's not about who's got the best ball-handling skills or who can make fifty perfect shots in a row. I made sure he learned."

"Made sure?"

"I pulled him out. Benched him. He was so mad at first. With all that time on the bench, though, he got a chance to see how the team played without him, and it made him realize that a team doesn't *need* a star player to be good. A team needs trust."

I'm speechless. My dad never mentioned this.

"His teammates all trusted each other, and they played just fine. Won a couple of the games, too. I only let him back on the court when he could tell me what *they* were doing right and *he* was doing wrong. Once he got back on the court, he was a totally different player. I see that same flaw in you now."

"What do you mean?"

"Mojo, you don't trust your team."

"That's because they're not trustworthy! George can't catch a single pass, Robin always gets the ball stolen, Terry—"

Coach Kit interrupts me by waving his hand around. "Stop, stop. All you're seeing in them is their flaws. I've seen them play. They're all good, but nervous. I think they can

90

probably tell that you don't believe in them. You need to *trust* them to be there for you, and they will be."

I feel cheated. Coach Kit isn't there on the court with us. He doesn't know what my teammates are like, or what playing with them is like. He doesn't know how Coach Ty can't get anybody to improve. It's definitely *not* my attitude that needs to change this time. It's our training methods.

"So that's it? That's all the help you're going to give me, after I ran around the city with you all day?" My hands tighten angrily on the ball I'm still holding. "This was *not* the agreement we had. You said you'd come coach the team."

"No, I said I'd help *you*. You were a good teammate for me today, and I liked working with you. I know you have it in you to be great. To be honest, Mojo, this is the only meaningful help I have for you. It's on you to decide what to do with it."

I glare at him across the court. He doesn't seem to care at all that I'm upset. I grit my teeth and start dribbling the ball, just for something to do.

"I'll think about it," I say. I don't like it, but I do wonder if there could be something true about what he's saying.

14

I spend all week thinking about what Coach Kit said, but by the time the next game rolls around, I still haven't decided if he's right. I practiced hard every day, but it felt like my teammates weren't trying the way I was. There's a difference between being able to catch a pass in practice versus catching one in an actual game, when it actually matters.

The stands for Hoops Academy aren't as full as they were at the start of the year. A lot of upperclassmen have decided we're not going to win, even though we've only played the first four games so far. I can't really blame them. I'm also not positive we're going to win, especially since this game is against the All-Stars, our biggest rivals. I bounce on the balls of my feet, sizing up our opponents. Even if my teammates aren't ready, I am.

I glance at George as we all take our positions on the court. Maybe I'll try what Coach Kit said and see if he can catch the ball. I feel like I never get a chance. By the end of the first quarter, we're down by six. It isn't as bad as some of our games, but I feel like we can barely keep our hands on the ball. I'm sweating through my jersey already, trying to be everywhere on the court at once. Whenever I try to score, there's an All-Stars player no matter which direction I turn.

Coach Ty tries to give us some plays during the quarter break, but I'm barely paying attention. As we break the huddle, I look up, and something in the stands catches my eye. Coach Kit is sitting in the second row, watching the game with a frown. I'm about to look away when he turns his head and looks straight at me. I'm reminded of standing in his backyard court, with him telling me that I don't trust my teammates.

Four minutes into the second quarter, the All-Stars have me trapped. Through a gap between two of them, I catch sight of George. He's unguarded, totally open on the other side of the court. He's not even looking at me. I stop dribbling the ball, and it's like the world goes into slow motion. George isn't looking at me because he knows I'm not going to pass to him. The whole team knows it. I've been trying to play this game all on my own, but look how that's worked out. With the way the other team is guarding me, there's no way I can score and we're eight points down now.

"George!" I shout, and he turns to look at me, surprised. He looks even more surprised when I pass the ball to him. It sails between the arms of the All-Stars players. A perfect pass. George reaches out, and for a moment I start to worry that I was wrong to pass it, that he'll drop it and the other team will take possession. Instead, he makes a perfect catch.

George snaps into motion, making a

break for the hoop at the other end of the court. The All-Stars turn and dash after him, but they're all too far away to catch him. He sinks the ball and the crowd cheers. I run toward George, shouting, "Yes!" at the top of my lungs as George stares at the scoreboard. "That was amazing!" I yell, throwing my arms around George.

The rest of the game gets even better. We match the All-Stars basket for basket and we even make up most of the point difference. Everybody's been playing hard, making passes and shots with a precision we've never had before. I'm a passing machine, going in for the all-time assist record. I'm so proud of all my teammates, but that feeling of wanting to *win* is back. We're so close! I can see the steely glint of determination in all my teammates' eyes. It's so different from the last game.

George catches my eye before the whistle blasts and we exchange a nod. Then like a shot, we're off. Terry snags the ball and tosses it to me. I make like I'm headed toward their basket, moving fast up the center of the court. Out of the corner of my eye, I see Jason running up the side, putting himself exactly where we planned he would. Just like I suspected, all the All-Stars converge on me.

I dodge them and make the pass to Jason. The other team switches direction, but they're not fast enough. Jason takes one step to reposition himself and shoots. The buzzer goes off right as the ball rolls off his fingers, and the entire gym seems to go silent as we watch it trace an arc through the air, spinning slightly. I'm worried that the spin will move it off course, but then the ball sinks through the net. I don't feel the reality of that moment until it hits the wooden floor of the court. We just got the two points we need to win.

I feel like the floor is shaking under my sneakers, and Jason flings his arms around me, screaming with excitement. As all my teammates pile into the hug, my eyes go over their heads, searching the stands. My parents are cheering and whistling, waving at me. I smile back at them, but I keep looking. Finally, I see Coach Kit. He's standing in his seat, clapping slowly.

The Hoops Academy fans flood out of the stands and crowd around us, celebrating our first victory of the season. My parents make their way through, smiles beaming brighter than the sun.

"I'm so proud of you!" Mom says, squeezing me tight.

"That was a really excellent game, Mojo," Dad says, and I feel like he means more than just my scoring.

I don't see Coach Kit again as the crowd disperses, and the whole time we're in the locker room, I'm disappointed that I didn't get to talk to him. He was right about everything, and following his advice got us our first win.

I find my parents waiting for me in the parking lot. "Hey," I call as I cross the asphalt toward them.

"Mojo, this is Coach Kit!" Dad says, stepping aside so I can see the person he's talking to. My face splits into a wide grin.

"Good teamwork out there, Mojo," Coach

Kit says. "I knew you could do it."

"Have you two talked?" Dad asks, looking between us in confusion.

"Oh, uh . . ." I hadn't told my parents about our adventure the previous weekend. I wanted to keep it to myself until I could decide what to do. It's time to come clean now, even though they might be upset that I didn't tell them earlier. "Yeah. Last weekend, I went to his house to ask him for help with basketball."

"Oh?" Dad raises an eyebrow.

"Well, you talk about him all the time, and with the way the team kept losing, and how much he had helped you in high school, I thought he might have some advice, you know, so we could start winning."

"I'm glad he did," Coach Kit says. "I think we both helped each other out a lot."

Mom and Dad glance between the two of us, then each other. "That's great," Dad says, putting a hand on Coach Kit's shoulder. "It's so good to see you again. We'll have to get together sometime to catch up. You can tell us all about what you two got up to last weekend."

"Over some basketball, of course," Coach Kit says.

Step onto the court with

HOOPS ACADEMY

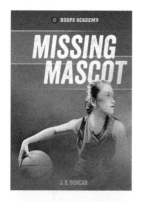
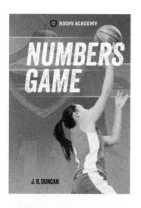

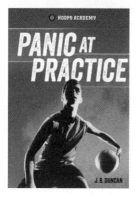